Praise for *Nothing in the World*:

T0162545

George Saunders:
"A beautiful, powerful book: mythic, vivid, heart-rending. Kesey reminds us anew of how much power there is in an open heart and the simple declarative sentence. He also reminds us that war is a viral madness, infecting everyone it touches."

Tom Bissell:
"Roy Kesey's Nothing in the World is as horrific and convincing as a nightmare. At its best it resembles the fever visions of Cormac McCarthy's *Child of God* or Denis Johnson's *Jesus' Son*. In telling the story of one young man caught up in the disintegration of Yugoslavia, Kesey has written a story that pushes us beyond war and strife. Instead, we are taken on a morally shattering forced march to the limits of human endurance itself. It is beautiful, brave, and I will not soon forget it."

Anthony Doerr:
Nothing in the World is a mesmerizing tale of expulsion and return: this is as much a trance as a story. Here's the Serbo-Croatian War as you've never seen it, its starkness and brutality balanced by the harrowing beauty of its landscapes. Roy Kesey is a fearless and very welcome new writer.

Laila Lalami:
"In haunting, evocative prose, Roy Kesey captures the horrors of war, the insanity of genocide, as well as the fleeting joys of love. *Nothing in the World* is a memorable debut."

David Vann:
"Roy Kesey is a natural story-teller, like the other Kesey, but writes about a wider world. This journey from an idyllic Croatian island life into the landscape of war is reminiscent of Cormac McCarthy's *Blood Meridian*— everything is taken away, and all that is terrifying is beautiful—but Kesey's writing also has the moral and figurative power of fairly tale. *Nothing In The World* will surprise you by how big it is."

Praise for *All Over*:

Laura Kasischke:
All Over is the strangest, best collection of stories you will read this year. With a seamless blend of lyricism and minimalism, Roy Kesey travels *All Over* the terrain of the psyche, the human condition, the relationships we have and fail to have. These stories team with insights, little horrors, moments of sweet verity, and surreal surprise. The characters are persuasive, and the storytelling is both hallucinatory and familiar. This is a new voice you must hear.

Cris Mazza:
Roy Kesey manifests his keen sense of human emotion not only in the sensual details of his fictions, but in their essential structures and narrative strategies. To say these fictions have breadth and depth is too shallow. These are three-dimensional affecting experiences wrought from prose.

Benjamin Percy:
These stories by Roy Kesey, in the way they brilliantly blend humor and pathos, remind me of coins tossed in the air, turning over and over, one side cast in light, the other in darkness. His writing is original, fearless, strikingly funny, and clean—so clean—his words sharp enough to cut the eye.

Chris Bachelder:
Roy Kesey tempers his prodigious imagination with fine syntactic control, so that his stories - like Donald Barthelme's - feel simultaneously free-wheeling and precise. *All Over* is an exhilarating collection - funny, harrowing, smart, odd, and inventive.

Lee K. Abbott:
For those keen to know the next generation of the American short story, consider *All Over*, which features the loopy paranoia of Don DeLillo, the po-mo-mo whimsy of Donald Barthelme, the spooky learnedness of Thomas Pynchon, the high-minded literary sleight-of-hand of Robert Coover and John Barth, and the secret geek speak of George Saunders. Add a touch of the Brothers Grimm, Jules Verne, and the Looney Tunes, and you've got a book of a million moving parts, all working in breathtaking harmony to keep illusion aloft.

Samantha Hunt:
Reading Roy Kesey is like being allowed to peep momentarily through a mysterious hole in the wall into a hidden universe that is very much like ours only slightly brighter, slightly sadder, certainly no less odd. Violinists play in the rain to keep swallows in flight. Strange, leaking packages tied up with string wait to be opened. In other words, Roy Kesey is a delight to read.

Peter Ho Davies:
"A restlessly inventive collection, as the best story collections so often are—comic and tender, ironic and earnest, deadpan and passionate. A distinctive new voice, from a distinctive new press."

Laird Hunt:
"Roy Kesey's *All Over* is intelligent, intense, often very funny and frequently, frankly, beautiful. Stories in this collection will appear in slightly different form in the deepest, darkest corners of your mind, where they will burn very, very brightly, for hours."

Michael Martone:
In *All Over*, Roy Kesey's postmodern parables are stunning mash-ups of style, content, characters. The book is a narrative train wreck that keeps happening of arcane jumbled juxtaposed graffitied rolling stock crashing into horribly hilarious verbal clown car kinetic sculpture.

NOTHING IN THE WORLD

1334 Woodbourne Street
Westland, MI 48186

www.dzancbooks.org

Published 2007 by Dzanc Books
Book design by Steven Seighman
Author photo by Lucy Cavender

07 08 09 10 11 5 4 3 2 1
First Edition October 2007

ISBN – 13: 978-0-9793123-2-8
ISBN – 10: 0-9793123-2-9

Printed in the United States of America

NOTHING IN THE WORLD

A Novella

by

Roy Kesey

For the four:

Svana, Bayo, Kijo, Moca

Puno hvala

The children were walled into the pier, for it could not be otherwise, but Rade, they say, had pity on them and left openings in the pier through which the unhappy mother could feed her sacrificed children. Those are the finely carved windows, narrow as loopholes, in which the wild doves now nest.
    - Ivo Andrić, *The Bridge on the Drina*

Because it matters what kind of emptiness is left behind by things or beings.
    - Milorad Pavić, *Landscape Painted With Tea*

Part I

1.

*T*he white stone walls of Joško's house were tinged gold in the growing light, and the only sound was the sharp ring of his father's pick glancing off rocks in the vineyard. Joško ran to join him as the sun slipped into the sky, and they worked together without speaking, his father freeing the rocks from the soil, Joško heaving them to his shoulder and staggering to the wall they were building to mark their property line to the east.

The dust began to rise as the sun burned off the dew. By the time his mother called that breakfast was ready, the vineyard was flooded with light, and sweat slicked Joško's neck and back. He walked to the shaded patio, turned on the faucet and took a drink from the hose.

Water spilled from the sides of his mouth, and Joško went still as two small blue butterflies came over the wall and settled at the edge of the puddle. He stared at them, thinking of nothing, then crouched down and clapped his hands around them, felt the faint beat of wings against his palms, parted his thumbs and peered inside and saw that his hands were empty.

❋

School went as usual: alone at lunch and during the breaks, invisible in the classroom. The teachers rarely called on Joško, and the few times he volunteered an answer, they looked at him as though they remembered having seen him before, but weren't quite sure where. His classmates didn't go out of their way to avoid him, but never sought him out or showed much interest in what he had to say. It was easier simply to be alone.

The last bell rang and Joško hurried home, put on his swimming suit, took up his fishing spear and headed into the hot low hills west of Jezera. The hillsides were patched with wild olive and fig trees, sage and thorn. At the top of a rise he caught another trail that led to a stone lookout. From there he could see the whole island of Murter, a severed finger of earth and heat, the Croatian mainland to one side and to the other the quiet sea.

Ten minutes later he arrived at the cliffs, and edged down through the striated rock. Boulders the size of tanks crowded the water that swirled over the tide pools and shifted away, and again he felt invisible, but here it was a source of strength. He worked back and forth along the shoreline, stopping short of every crevice, dropping down and crawling forward, careful to keep his shadow from falling across the water.

No one else in his family was any good at spearfishing, but it had never seemed difficult to Joško. It was simply a question of knowing where to go and how to get there, and of not missing when the moment came. Though he would never have admitted it to anyone, at times he tossed dying fish back into the water, throwing his spear again and again for the pleasure of hitting what he aimed at.

Three fat sea bass now hung from the stringer on his belt. He set his spear in a cleft in the rocks and hooked the stringer over its tip, drew a cloth from his waistband and wound it around his right hand. The periška that lived in the sand of the sea floor were by far his favorite food, but the edges of their long ochre shells left wounds that took weeks to heal.

He watched the sun settle into a thin bank of clouds on the horizon, then stepped out onto a ledge and dove into the water. The deeper currents thrashed and curled. He kept at it, dive after dive, until his shell-bag was so heavy that he could barely make it back to the surface.

He checked the tide pools for abalone shells for his sister, and found only one. It was almost four inches across, too big for the earrings and brooches that Klara made, and the inner surface was already weathered and dull. He tucked it into his bag all the same, climbed up the cliff, and now the wind strengthened. The Adriatic whorled into the coastline, small waves spiking and guttering below. Shade by shade the sky turned his favorite color, a ridged blue-gray as solid as stone.

He returned to his house, and its red slate roof glowed under the streetlights, and there were grapes and cantaloupes in a basket on the patio. As he washed the salt from his body, his mother came up the sidewalk, back from the market where old women waited with their twined bunches of rosemary and dill. She took the fish and the periška, and Joško went to Klara's bedroom. The pile of abalone shells in the corner was almost a meter high and smelled of rot. His parents complained from time to time, but he always insisted that sooner or later she would come back, would need the shells, would use every single one.

He went to the kitchen, opened the periška and cut out the meat while his mother cleaned the fish. He watched as she fried everything in olive oil. Then they all sat down at the table, and after his mother had prayed they began to eat, wiping up the grease with slices of bread, drinking wine from rough wooden pots.

When the dishes were cleared, Joško's father turned on the television. The news was the usual mix of referendums and local elections, arguments about conditions in Kosovo and the Vojvodina now that they'd been swallowed again by Serbia, and discussions of Slovenia's recent freedom after three short days of fighting. His father said that he couldn't understand what was happening, that all Yugo-slavs were supposed to be brothers. His mother said that that hadn't been true since Tito died, and that the Serbs were not to be trusted under any circumstances.

They both looked at Joško, and he smiled and shrugged. These were the same arguments he heard most days in history class, and they meant nothing more to him here than there. He suspected he'd have trouble trusting a Serb if he ever met one, but couldn't say he spent much time thinking about them. While his parents had been talking he'd been wondering what Klara was doing just now.

Two years ago she would have been in her bedroom, putting on her make-up and choosing her clothes, preparing to join her friends at one of the cafes or bars in the center of town. Then she met a man from the south. A few weeks later she married him for reasons no one could understand, and went to live with him in Dubrovnik. She hadn't been back to Jezera in months.

Joško had done what he could to fill the small holes that Klara's absence carved in his chest. He spent most of his free time working the bit of vineyard that his father had given him the day he turned fifteen. Pruning, sulfur-dusting, harvest and rest, then pruning again: the future had seeped into the past like water into dry soil.

As Joško leafed through a comic book, his father turned the television off, took an old mandolin from its case, and his mother sang the songs he had been hearing since birth, of the sea and the sand and Bura, the wind from the north. If Klara had been there it would have been perfect.

At last his parents went to bed, and Joško took his father's car into town. He sat down on the terrace of his favorite bar, sipped his beer and watched the girls from nearby villages who'd come to show off their sundresses and their long dark legs. The girls ignored him as they always had. Then he heard a radio broadcast turned up, and someone in the bar said, It's finally begun.

2.

For the first time in his life, Joško had someone to hate. Serb guerrillas had attacked in the Krajina, and the federal army had helped them crush the towns of Tenja and Dalj. They'd started in Western Slavonia as well, only sixty kilometers from Zagreb. Now he stood outside the post office, waiting in line with several dozen other young men. He knew some of them from school—one was in his geometry class—but could think of nothing to add to their conversation. Their faces blurred in the heat, and there was a slight vibration in the air that he could not identify.

His decision to enlist had not really been a decision at all. He'd returned home from the bar, and his parents were awake, and the television was on again. His parents had looked at him, and he had known: he would sign up and fight for the Motherland and probably die. His father had been silent as his mother spoke on and on. Joško hadn't heard any of the words, and didn't need to.

A sergeant measured him, gave him a uniform, and waved him to a shed where he picked up a rucksack complete with the things that would apparently be necessary—a canteen, a compass, a knife, a sewing kit and a tin of waterproof matches. He was sent to stand in another line, and the vibration in the air grew stronger. Then he realized that it was the sound of his own fear, and he had no idea what to do about it, no idea how to make it stop.

He balled up his fists, spoke to no one, kept his eyes on the ground. His fear grew louder and louder in his head, and he stumbled as he stepped to the head of the line. The soldier there said something he didn't catch, and handed him an AK-47. It was old but well oiled and clean, felt perfectly right in his hands, and suddenly Joško could hear again. He asked the soldier to show him how to load it. The man said he'd learn that soon enough, and pointed him toward a jeep.

There were two other new soldiers already sitting in the back seat. Joško asked where the three of them were headed, and what would be expected of them, and when they'd be allowed to visit home, but the other soldiers didn't know anything either. They all sat there waiting. Then an older soldier came over, climbed into the driver's seat and told them to shut the hell up, though no one had been talking.

It was only a few minutes' drive to Tijesno and the narrow bridge connecting Murter to the mainland. The jeep jolted across the concrete slabs edged slightly out of square, sped up when they hit the roadway, and twenty minutes later they were at Tribunj. The driver told the other two soldiers to get their gear, find the main square, and wait for the rest of their squad.

The road curled and cut southwest along the coast. The heat seeped into Joško's lungs, made his chest heavy and slow. He slumped in his seat. The noise of the engine was a low ache, a faraway gnashing of teeth.

Then the older soldier was pushing him out of the jeep, yelling for him to grab his rifle and rucksack and get moving. They were stopped under a torn awning stretched out from a bus station. A hand-painted sign hanging over the door read "Šibenik" in black letters half a meter high. Joško gathered his things and asked where he was supposed to go. The driver pointed toward the beach and drove off.

Joško stepped into the furrowed sunlight. Across the street was a vast mound of brick and charred beams. To his right was a plywood kiosk, its counter lined with wristwatches and soap, and behind the kiosk was an empty bench.

All Joško really wanted was to sit down, but then an old man came walking up, rubbing his hands together. He stopped to look at Joško, at the ground in front of him, at the air halfway between them.

His hands were still working, still cleaning. He came closer, stroked the rucksack as if it were a small deer, and asked a question that Joško couldn't understand—the man's words weren't really words, just sounds. Joško shook his head, and the man leaned forward, shouted the question as if the answer might save him from something.

Joško turned and ran to the beach. A hundred meters north was a small army camp, and waiting there were the five other men of his squad. Joško asked Dražen, the squad captain, which branch of the army they were in. Dražen said that it wasn't yet clear, but he would let the men know as soon as he found out. The other men looked at Joško, and looked away.

✳

No one in the squad had seen combat, but two of them had done hitches with the Yugoslav army years before. In the mornings Dražen taught weapons handling and marksmanship, and in the afternoons Vlade taught demolitions and recon, not because they were experts in these areas but because it was all that they remembered. Joško struggled with everything but shooting: he could hit targets so small and so distant that the other soldiers could hardly see them.

In the evenings he became invisible again. They all cleaned their rifles—Joško's favorite part of each day, the smell of the oil, the soft cloth, the cold metal components sliding precisely into place—and when they were done the others played poker while he listened to the news that flowed from the radio. One town after another was shattered by the Serb tanks, and when the siege of Vukovar began, arguments among the other soldiers over whether the city would fall turned into fistfights. Busload after busload of refugees arrived on the coast, and Joško watched them go by, the pale faces framed like portraits in the windows.

Then a pair of Serb jets found their way to Šibenik, and Dražen informed the men that they had been assigned to anti-aircraft duty. Every evening the jets flew low over the city, and every morning crowds gathered for work crews and funerals. When the cemeteries were full, graves began to appear in careful lines along the edges of parks and playgrounds.

For the first few days of this, Joško and the others could do nothing but lie on their backs and shoot up at the planes with their rifles. At last they heard that an air defense system was on its way, and they congratulated each other in advance for saving the city.

What arrived the next week was a single 88mm, a relic from World War II, its barrel pitted with rust inside and out. Along with the gun came a German mercenary to teach them how it worked. He was tall and pale, and a thin scar split his face lengthwise, running from below his right eye down into his thick brown mustache, beginning again in his bottom lip, slipping to the point of his chin.

According to the German, in addition to being in poor condition, the 88 would be almost useless against modern jets, particularly with no searchlights and no radar. The sound locator was broken and no parts were available to fix it. Also, the gun was designed for a crew of eight, so some of the men would have to do two jobs.

The German assigned them their positions: Joško laying for elevation and line, Bakalar loading and firing, Mladen on the predictor and Vlade handling ammunition, Papiga setting range and Dražen setting vertical deflection. They practiced for hours with empty shells. The gun could fire twenty rounds a minute, but they'd only have ten or twelve seconds before the jets were out of range.

That evening, as the jets leveled off to drop their bombs, Joško's squad fired three shots as quickly as they could. High above there were puffs of greasy black encasing small flares of red. The noise made Joško's head ring, and the jets flew away.

❋

The sun lowered into the sea, and Joško watched a giant cloud become a whale, and then a musk ox, and then a bear. He fingered the abalone shell that hung on a leather thong around his neck, a gift from Klara, who had written from Dubrovnik when she heard that he'd joined the army. He was almost certain it was a shell they'd found together one morning when they were very young. It was perfectly round, and its pearled inner surface was a rare translucent swirl of violet and green.

8

He remembered the day he'd left Jezera, the scene on the porch of his house—his mother crying as she told him how proud she was, his father twisting a newspaper tighter and tighter until it came apart in his hands—and his cheek began to twitch. He waited to see if the twitching would stop on its own. When it didn't, he took the shell and rubbed his dancing cheek until it quieted.

The mercenary stood off to the side of camp, smoking one hand-rolled cigarette after another. Dražen was manning the binoculars, and the other soldiers were stretched out flat on their backs in the sand. They stared up at the reddening sky as they worked through the latest rumor, that a shipment of Stingers had been deployed with squads roving the coast, waiting for the chance to bring down a jet.

Dražen handed the binoculars to Vlade, and the men's talk shifted to stories of women they'd been with. When it became clear to Joško that he wasn't going to learn anything helpful, he started thinking of his sister and her friends in Jezera. Klara's long straight hair, Marijana's deep black eyes, Andrea's legs. Nataša's breasts and Maja's voice and...

Of course, none of Klara's friends had ever paid any attention to him. Joško watched as Papiga got up and began hopping from boulder to boulder, his arms spread like wings. The conversation turned to football, and Bakalar started in on Dinamo Zagreb and their chances once the war was—

- How about if all of you shut the fuck up?

It was the German. He walked from soldier to soldier, staring at each of them. Joško tried to remember the man's name, and realized that he'd never told them.

- I do not understand you. We all know that I am here for the money, that my paycheck comes each month no matter who is winning or losing, no matter who lives or dies, but you...

He shook his head, and took his time rolling a cigarette.

- How much are they paying you? Dražen asked.

The mercenary laughed. He looked at Dražen, and finally shrugged.

- The money's not bad. Not as good as in Angola, but not bad.

He turned to Papiga.

- I'll bet you don't even know who I was fighting against there.
- The government?
- Of course, but who else?

Papiga guessed Namibians. They were the wrong answer.

- Cubans, the mercenary said. Very good soldiers. Very smart. It was a good war.
- A good war.
- Yes.
- What, exactly—
- When both sides are the same. Both have good weapons, good soldiers, and the smartest man is who wins.
- Did you win? Joško asked. In Angola?

The mercenary looked away and smiled.

- The government has offered to stop fighting, and Savimbi will accept. Does this mean the war is over? I don't know. But while I was there I won nine thousand dollars each month. And I am not dead.

Bakalar laughed, called to Vlade that once the war in Croatia was over they should sign up for Africa.

- You will all be dead before this war is over, the mercenary said.

He started walking in circles again, not staring at anyone now.

- You understand, yes, that this is not a good war? It is a terrible war. The Serbs have solid equipment, thorough training. I have garbage like this 88, and to operate the garbage, instead of soldiers I have children and old men. You argue about women, you argue about football, you argue about whether Vukovar will fall. Of course Vukovar will fall. It will hold on as long as it can, and then it will fall. I was there, you know, at the beginning. One time a boy, maybe fifteen years old, is the only one I have left. He is not so smart so I tell him things simply: I say, 'Look, I need the big gun from those dead men over there.' He does not wait for me to tell him how to go. He just runs. Bullets are everywhere. He gets to the bunker and picks up the Browning. He cannot run fast with it, and I yell for him to wait. He runs back without waiting.

- So he made it? said Mladen.

- Yes. But he did not bring the ammunition. I tell him we need the big bullets for the big gun, and to wait for my signal. He says he does not need to wait because he is very lucky. He runs again to the bunker, gets the ammunition and runs back, all the time with the Serbs shooting at him.

- Lucky kid.

- Not so lucky. He was killed the next day. Brave, yes, but not so smart and not so lucky. In war, if you are stupid, if you do not listen to me, you will die. And if you are not stupid, and you listen to me carefully, you will probably also die, but maybe your country will survive.

＊

In the morning the mercenary sat them down and said that it was time for them to learn infantry tactics and sniping. Vlade asked why an anti-aircraft squad needed to know infantry maneuvers. The German stared at him, then pointed at the nearest ridge and said that sixty Serb tanks and a thousand foot-soldiers would be arriving in two or three weeks to answer his question.

The mercenary brought out a roll of maps and spread them one by one across the ground. He spent the next hour asking the men how they would attack a given target, and ridiculing their answers.

- You speak as if there will be no one defending the trench. There will be many, you understand? They are something you must get past, like a river, and you kill them like building a bridge. Whoever builds their bridges fastest, to the best places, that is who wins.

They drilled for twelve hours, the German screaming each time someone hesitated or fumbled a piece of equipment. There was no break for lunch, and none for dinner, but his shouts and insults thinned out as the evening wore on. At last he told them that if they continued to drill like that, someday they would be soldiers.

Joško ate his rations, washed his face, and sat down alone on the beach. He was searching the sky for Venus when the German came and sat beside him. The man rolled a cigarette, lit it and lay back. Joško cleared his throat.

- What we are doing here is pointless, isn't it.

- With the 88? Yes. But most of what is done in most wars is pointless.

- I wish I was somewhere I could use my rifle.

- So do I. You are shit at everything else, but if I could find you a proper weapon and get you out on special missions... Anyway, it doesn't matter. With the way the Serbs are advancing, it won't be long.

Joško stared at the sea, wondering, and finally asked the man how long he'd been a mercenary.

- Sixteen years.
- And when will you stop?
- I will fight only four years more.
- Why four?
- That is when I will have enough money not to fight anymore.

The German seemed suddenly very tired and very happy. Joško thought of Jezera, of Klara, of how far things were away. He looked back at the mercenary, and the man's eyes were closed; his cigarette was almost gone, and ashes littered his uniform. Then the coal burned into his bottom lip and he woke shouting, spitting the heat away. He pressed his hand to his mouth and looked at his fingers carefully, studying the spittle like tea leaves. He laughed, and held out his hand for Joško to see.

- Do you know what this pain is?

Joško shook his head.

- This is paying for what you do not have. It does not matter if there is rain or sun. The men put vinegar on the sponge and lift it to you, but it doesn't help the pain.

Joško looked around. Papiga had the binoculars, and the other soldiers were talking quietly as they cleaned their equipment.

- Do you understand? the man asked.

- Not really.

- You will.

Papiga shouted that the jets were coming, and Joško was the first to his feet but slipped in the sand and was the last into position. He flinched as the gun fired, and stared at the jet that staggered, stalled, and arced into the sea.

They heard the remaining jet coming back, and Bakalar slammed another shell into the breech. The jet passed overhead, the gun fired, a wing folded and the jet flamed and dropped.

- Both of them! Joško screamed. We got both of them!

He threw back his head and howled, the pleasure of it, his throat went tight and the darkness fragmented and spun.

3.

The next morning the German was gone. He'd left a note taped to the 88 warning that more jets would be coming, and they would no longer fly in so low. In a nearly illegible postscript he'd added that he now knew he'd been wrong, that Dražen and his men were excellent soldiers, that Croatia was lucky to have them and they would be fine as long as they didn't do stupid things.

Vlade and Bakalar took turns reliving the night before and reminding Joško that he'd passed out just as the celebration started. Then a group of reporters arrived and informed them that they were the first heroes the war had produced. Most of the interviews that followed started with variations on one basic question: How had it felt to send those bastards to the pits that waited for them in hell? The other soldiers talked about duty and justice and freedom, but when Joško's turn came, the hair rose on the back of his neck, and the only answer that occurred to him was, There's nothing like hitting what you aim at.

A few hours later the reporters threw their equipment into their cars and sped away. Papiga blamed Joško for not giving better answers, and Mladen was convinced that a major offensive was about to be launched somewhere in the northeast, but Bakalar had heard from a cameraman that one of the army's roving squads had been nearby when the two jets went down, and that in fact their Stingers had made the kills.

While the others argued about who should be getting the credit, Joško reread a postcard that had arrived from Klara that morning. It said that she hoped he would soon be sent to Dubrovnik to protect her from the Serb ships that were shelling her beautiful old city. The postcard didn't mention her husband. Joško had already asked Dražen a dozen times if he could be transferred south. The answer was that Dražen didn't know how the transfer process worked, or even if there was one, and that if Joško abandoned his post he would be hunted down.

❋

The air attacks on Šibenik ceased, but over the course of the next week part of the Serb army moved in through Bosnia to attack central Croatia and split the country in two. They took a swath from the eastern border to within shelling range of the coast, and from Gračac in the north to Sinj in the south. Dražen spent hours each day on the phone, begging for reinforcements and trying to find someone who could show them how to reconfigure the 88 as an anti-tank weapon. He always hung up hollow-eyed and hoarse.

One morning a courier arrived from Zagreb with a crate and a sealed directive. Dražen read the directive, pried the lid off the crate, and called for everyone to take out their plastic ID cards.

Joško handed over his card, and Dražen gave him a set of dog-tags and a box bearing his name. Back at his cot Joško set the tags on his pillow and took out his knife. Inside the box he found a bottle of rakija, three bars of chocolate, a carton of cigarettes, a plastic case and a fat white envelope. In the envelope was a sheaf of money bound with a rubber band, and a letter from the President of Croatia. The letter began,

Valiant and Distinguished Soldier:

Your role in the defense of the Motherland will not be forgotten when the history of this glorious war is written. Your courage and selfless sacrifice...

Joško scratched at the previous night's mosquito bites—one on each shoulder, another on his forehead and a cluster below his navel. He read the letter twice, then took out the sheaf of money and counted it. It came to almost fifty thousand dinar. He liked the sound of the number, though it wouldn't buy much. Perhaps he'd get a new set of clothes for the party his parents would give once the war was over and he was home again.

Inside the plastic case was a medal. It was large and thick, but not very heavy, made of something not quite like gold. On the front were the words "Medal of Honor" and an imprint of the Croatian flag. The back was almost smooth.

Joško wondered if he really was a hero, if the girls in the cafes would now stop to talk with him, if his teachers would remember his name. He didn't feel particularly heroic. Something else was needed, he thought—something bigger. Maybe if he could track down the German, learn from him, get chosen for a special mission or two...

As he put the medal back in its case, Joško thought he heard a noise, something like the buzzing of a mosquito, but thinner, and very far away. Papiga and Bakalar had opened their bottles of rakija, were competing to see who would finish first, and Vlade was clapping, urging them on. Joško tucked the plastic case into the box and got to his feet. Perhaps the noise was coming from the radio.

The sky was not cloudless but bright, and the sea was quiet, almost asleep. He walked down to the beach, and saw a large gray seashell that hadn't been there the day before. Could the wind cause such a sound, playing through the shell somehow? But there was no wind. He picked the shell up, walked back toward his cot, and a white flare filled his mind, a surge of heat lifted him off the ground, a roar like the birth of a world carried him away.

❄

Joško opened his eyes, and the sky was a thin whitish blue. There was the warm salty sweetness of blood in his mouth, and behind his eyes he felt a strange dense presence. He raised one hand to his head. Above his left ear, a shard of metal protruded from his skull. He wrapped his hand around it and ripped it out. Pain deafened him, and strips of sky floated down to enfold him.

He opened his eyes again, and now light from a lopsided moon sifted around him. He lay perfectly still, trying to understand what had happened, and then, of course—more jets had come.

Joško looked down at his legs. They didn't seem to be injured. He drew his knees to his chest and ran his hands from his hips to his ankles. Not much pain, no broken bones. He touched the side of his head softly, his fingers tracing the edge of the hole, then stopped, afraid of touching his brain.

He rolled over and got to his knees, squinted through the silty darkness, and on the canvas of a mangled cot beside him there was a single arm. It was silver, almost white in the moonlight, and there were no rings on the fingers of its hand. He stood carefully, and picked the arm up. It had been torn off above the elbow, and the severed end was black and shredded. He wondered whose it was. Then he saw a soldier lying face down in the rubble, stretched out as if diving into the earth.

Joško turned the man over, and it was Bakalar, his moustache limp over broken teeth. Both of his arms were still attached. His eyes were open, and on his face was the expression of a man holding very good cards.

He left Bakalar staring up at the sky, and one by one he found the other soldiers. Papiga was curled up like a bird that had flown into a window; there was no blood on his face, but Joško could not wake him. Vlade was splayed and twisted, a piece of metal tubing driven through his stomach, out the small of his back and into the ground. Mladen was draped over the low stone wall on the east side of camp, his jaw hanging away from his face. And near the ruptured water barrel, Joško found Dražen lying loose-boned in the sand. He looked comfortable, though his right arm was missing. Joško remembered what he was carrying, dusted the arm off and set it in place. It seemed to fit. This relieved Joško immeasurably.

He headed back through the camp, hoping to find the things he was responsible for. In the wreckage where his cot had been he found his rifle, but the barrel was bent, and after trying to twist it back into shape he gave up and let it fall. He scrabbled around for his new metal tags and couldn't find them anywhere, but he did find his rucksack and the box he had received from the President.

The bottle of rakija had shattered. Joško started to cry as he pulled the pieces of glass from the box and flung them at the sea. He dried the letter as best he could, but the President's signature was smeared, unrecognizable.

Then he heard a faint song. At first he thought it was Klara singing to him from Dubrovnik—the voice was so similar to hers, so rich with love and so distant—but there were inflections he'd never heard before, and this voice came from somewhere to the east.

He listened carefully as he stuffed his possessions back into his rucksack and took one last look around the camp. Near Mladen's body was another rifle, this one undamaged. Joško slung it over his shoulder, and decided that nothing more needed to be done.

4.

Joško followed the girl's voice deeper and deeper into the night. She sang ballads and folk songs and at times only his name, and he wondered if she was beautiful. He skirted the few towns he came to and crossed all roads at a run. The moon slipped below the horizon, and a few hours later the sky began to glow.

As the sun rose over a range of hills in the distance, Joško entered the mouth of a shallow valley. There was a grove of willows whose thin leaves twisted like the fingers of the deaf. He rested for a moment in the shade, and the girl's voice faded away.

There was now no sound except for the wind. He started walking again, and his cheek began to twitch. He slowed his pace so that the twitching was more or less in time with his steps. Then across a draw he saw the dark green of a pear orchard, and realized that his stomach was burning with hunger.

He crossed the draw and entered the orchard, picked a pear from a low branch, bit into it, and his whole spindly body sang with the flavor. He finished the pear in two more bites, and was about to pick another when he heard someone shout.

He turned, and on the far side of the orchard he saw a small stone house. There was more shouting, and the door swung open. Out came an old man waving a long stick.

- Dog! the man shouted. Mongrel! What makes you think you can—

Joško cocked his rifle and brought it to his shoulder, and the old man grew young, his stick was a rifle too and Joško shot him in the head. The man fell simply. Joško ate three more pears, put half a dozen into his bandana, gathered the corners together and tied the bulging pouch to his belt.

❋

Late that afternoon Joško came to a creek, and stopped only long enough to fill his canteen. The girl's voice had not yet returned, and he was starting to worry. He waded quickly across and walked into a field of wild poppies. The flowers shifted around him, and it felt as though he were bathing in their color.

The field ended at the base of a steep shale hill. It was a long climb to the ridgeline, and from there he saw a string of mountains in front of him, and another beyond that. Waiting for his lungs to calm, he looked downhill, and saw a ditch where three Croatian soldiers were huddled together. All three were waving their arms, and one shouted, Get down!

Joško hurried off the ridge and crawled in alongside them. The nearest soldier had fouled his pants, and the odor curled around him.

- Is it true? he asked Joško. Is it him?

- What?

- The sniper! said another. Is it Hadžihafizbegović?

- What sniper?

- For fuck's sake! the third one said. The one who's shooting at us!

Joško peered over the top of the ditch, and saw a dead soldier stretched out in the dirt not far away.

- From six hundred meters! said the soldier who stank. Six hundred meters, and he shot Marko right in the ear!

- An artist! said the second.

- We aren't sure it's Hadžihafizbegović, said the third, but we heard that he's around here somewhere, and the Muslims have no one else who shoots so well.

- The Muslims? Joško said. Are we fighting them, too?

- Not officially. But there have been incidents.

- Like what?

- You know, people getting carried away.

- Oh. Well, I'm sorry about your friend.

- That's okay, said the first. He was an asshole.

After the men had introduced themselves, the second soldier looked at Joško's uniform and asked, What unit are you with?

- It's a special mission, Joško said.

Now all three soldiers were staring at him, so he gazed at the horizon and asked how long they'd been hiding in the ditch.

- Half an hour or so, said the third. How can we move?

- And where is the sniper?

The first soldier pointed across the canyon to a sharp peak.

- You can stay here with us if you want, said the second. There's no point in making a run for it until dark. What happened to your head?

Joško smiled, rooted through his rucksack, and pulled out his three bars of chocolate. They were nearly melted, and he apologized as he handed one to each of the men. Then he got to his feet and ran back uphill.

- Where are you going? called the third soldier.

Joško didn't answer. He crossed the ridge and followed it north for a thousand meters or so, came back across and ran for the valley floor. He headed up the opposite side, crawled not quite to the top, made his way back south a few hundred meters, and stopped to catch his breath and remove his boots.

He stayed low in the brush until he reached the side of the peak to which the soldier had pointed, then threaded his way up through the tall grass. Near the top, he slowed and became a shadow. Stone to stone, invisible now. A step at a time. Above him, the sky was fading to the blue-gray he'd always loved.

He crawled over the crest, and found a large boulder split in two. Between its halves the grass was pressed flat. He looked down the slope beyond and up the following hillside, and there was a flicker of movement at the skyline.

Joško ran down into the draw and pushed up the far side, down the next slope and up again, quietly over the top, and three hundred meters below him was a soldier in a strange gray uniform hunched beneath a twisted oak. Joško waited, and when the man stood Joško shot him twice in the back.

The man fell. Joško watched for a moment before walking down the hill. Twenty meters away he stopped to watch again. The man did not move. Joško closed in slowly, saw the man's hand twitch, flipped him over and closed his thumbs across the man's throat. He held on until the convulsions stopped, then remembered what he had meant to ask.

- Are you Hadžihafizbegović?

The corpse did not respond. Joško glanced at where his thumbs had been, and their outlines were clear in the man's dark flesh. Like two trains passing each other late at night, he thought. Lovely. He looked at the oak, and wondered what would be made from her when she was cut down. Farther down the hill stood another oak, his branches bare and trembling, and Joško started to cry. He was still crying when he noticed the thick gold ring in the sniper's left ear.

I could melt it down, Joško thought, and make something for the girl, something beautiful. He pulled at the earring, but it held as though welded on. He wiped his tears away and punched the corpse in the face, then thought of a very funny joke he could play at some point. He laughed, lifted the head of the soldier who might or might not have been Hadžihafizbegović, and pulled out his knife.

- It's all taken care of, Joško shouted through the dusk.

His voice limped back to him from all sides, scraped hollow by the distance.

- What happened? one of the soldiers shouted back.

- Nothing. Everything's fine.

Silhouettes came into view on the ridgeline.

- Are you sure? yelled another.

- I told you, I took care of everything. There's nothing to worry about. Go home.

- You killed him? You killed Hadžihafizbegović?

- Are you sure that's who it was?

- Of course! Who else could it have been?

Joško had no answer, and was getting a little tired of all the shouting. He waved, and one short arm waved back. Then he headed down the ridge to find his boots and pick the burrs out of his socks before it got any darker.

*

The girl's voice was back, not quite as distant as before but less distinct, and she was no longer singing. Instead she was telling a story that Joško had trouble following—something about scorpions, and something about men with metal hands.

The story ended and the voice faded again. The moon hung almost full in the sky. If it had been perfectly white Joško could have stopped walking and stared up at it forever, but the scars on its face scared him, and he kept his eyes down as he climbed one ridge after another.

When he stopped to rest at the top of the steepest ridge yet, he felt a slight wetness on his right thigh. He opened his bandana, and saw that the pears had been crushed. He lobbed them down the hill like grenades, and immediately regretted it: his hunger was a small animal chewing at his stomach. Worse still, his throat was tight with thirst, and his canteen was empty. He trudged five or six kilometers more, picking his way up and down the blue-black hills. He crossed one last ridge, and before him the earth stretched out flat and luminescent.

Perhaps two kilometers away he saw a pattern in the darkness, square black patches at regular intervals against a grayer background. He hurried toward it, and as he lost altitude it disappeared.

He walked on steadily, and the black patches returned, took on strength and depth, became the houses of a small town. Joško wondered why there were no lights on anywhere. It wasn't possible for everyone in the town already to be asleep—sunset hadn't been so long ago. Then again, time was no longer what it had been. Before, it splintered easily into hours and minutes, but now it was a dense vastness around him, contracting and expanding erratically, the heart of a dying giant.

The houses were unlike any he had seen before. Their roofs were four-sided pyramids of dull black slate, and the windows were three long narrow panes mounted side by side in heavy frames. He searched one street after another for a cafe or restaurant, and found nothing. He circled in toward the center of town, thinking he might find someone still awake who could at least give him some bread and a mouthful of water, but here most of the houses had been shelled and leaned sadly like old skulls.

In the middle of the road was a crater lined with broken glass, and he blanched at a memory of his camp. The jets had broken it. Or scrambled it, he thought, turned it into a child's game, a puzzle to be put back together, and surely someone was already at work burying his friends and gathering the pieces of the 88.

He skirted the hole, and through the front window of a nearby house he thought he saw a flicker of light. Taking care not to disturb the muddy pair of shoes on the step, he knocked at the sagging door. There was a long silence, and footsteps, but the door did not open. He tried the knob but the door was locked. He kicked the door open, and inside was a young woman. Her long black hair was parted in the middle just like Klara's, her mouth looked as though it were made for singing, and Joško thought he had found her, the girl who would love him forever.

She let out a cry and tried to push him back through the door, but Joško caught her wrists. When she calmed slightly he let her go. The girl walked to a wooden table that held a small oil lamp, sat down and folded her arms across her chest.

- Come in, she said. Take whatever you want. There is nothing here that has not already been taken at least once.

- Are you—

But the girl's voice was wrong, her accent too rough and weighted for singing the songs he had heard.

- Well, said the girl, what are you waiting for?

The many colors of her blouse were no longer bright, and she was wearing strange pants that billowed away from her legs. Her teeth were stained, and one side of her jaw was bruised and swollen.

- Whenever you're ready, she said.

Joško's cheek began to twitch.

- Don't worry, he said. I'm not a mongrel. I'm just looking for something to eat.

The girl said nothing. Joško set down his rucksack and leaned his gun against the doorjamb.

- Besides, he said, if I hurt you, you would scream, and the others would come.

From the girl came a sound that was almost a laugh.

- What others?

- The others in the village.

- There are no others in the village. And even if there were, they wouldn't come.

- Why not?

The girl closed her eyes.

- Why would I want to hurt you? Joško said.

- For the same reason your brothers did. Because you can.

- But look at me. I'm no bigger than you are.

- And poison is kept in small bottles.

Joško went to the nearest cupboard. There was nothing in it but an old copy of the Quran, its cover faded and curling at the corners. He closed the cupboard door harder than he meant to, and the girl jumped.

- All you want is food? she asked.

- That's all I want.

- And if I give you some, you'll go away?

- Yes.

The girl stared at him, got up and walked into the darkness at the back of the house. Joško massaged his cheek. He heard the sound of something heavy being dragged across the floor, and the creak of boards being lifted. When the girl returned she was carrying a small basket of bread and potatoes.

- If you won't hurt me, you can have it all.

Joško nodded, and she went to a shelf and took down a dusty plate webbed with yellow cracks. She wiped it clean, took a paring knife from a drawer and began peeling the potatoes. Joško sat down and watched her. She arranged the slices of potato in a fan around the plate, and put a large piece of bread in the center.

- There, she said. Your feast is ready.

- You aren't going to cook the potatoes?

The girl's face went tight.

- Cook them with what? With electricity from the dam your brothers blew up? Or with the kerosene they used to burn down our mosque?

Joško said that he was sorry. The girl did not respond. He picked up one of the potato slices, took a bite, and asked for a glass of water.

The girl rubbed her eyes, took a glass from the shelf, filled it from a cistern in the corner. Joško thanked her, and drank the water in three long gulps. He put the glass down and burped, covering his mouth a moment too late.

- You really aren't going to hurt me? the girl asked.

- Of course not.

She got him another glass of water, hesitated, leaned over and looked at the side of his head.

- It's okay, Joško said. It doesn't hurt at all.

- How did it happen?

He tried to remember, but now nothing was clear.

- I'm not sure. Something about an arm.

He drank the glass of water and wiped his mouth. The girl took a rag from the sink and soaked it in the cistern. She began to rub at the edges of the hole, and Joško winced at each stroke.

- I don't have any medicine.

Joško nodded, and the girl put down the rag, ran her hands through her hair.

- Where are you going to sleep tonight?

- I don't know.

He fetched himself a third glass of water, and his cheek began to calm.

- You can stay here with me if you like.

The wind soughed in the trees outside. Joško tried to think of reasons to stay, or not to stay, and came up with none.

- All right. Thank you.

- Wait here.

The girl went to the back room and returned with a shallow metal pan. She filled it halfway, took the rag from the counter and the lamp from the table, and disappeared again. Joško sat in the darkness, heard the whispering of cloth, and walked to the doorway to look. To one side was a small bed, and the girl was

25

standing naked in the center of the room. Light from the oil lamp licked across her face.

- I told you to wait, she said.

Joško took the rag from her hand, and traced back and forth across her shadowed back.

❋

All night he'd listened to the sound of the wind clawing at the door. Now the girl woke, kissed him, put her hands to the sides of his face.

- It's okay, she said.

But it wasn't okay. The other girl, the one who had sung for him, would she even want him anymore? And what would Klara think?

Klara. He took off his necklace, stared at the shell. Now he could finally protect her like he should have done from the start.

Joško pushed the girl gently away and began searching for his clothes. The girl got up and left the room. When he came into the kitchen she was filling his canteen. She tightened the cap and wiped the canteen dry, handed it to him and pointed to a plastic bag on the table.

Inside the bag were two potatoes and a large piece of bread. He thanked her, hooked the canteen to his belt and shouldered his rucksack and rifle.

The girl glanced down at the floor. There was a small pool of dried blood where the rucksack had been.

- I'm sorry, Joško said. Do you want me to clean it up?

The girl backed into a corner.

- No. Just go away.

He nodded and opened the door. Daylight slipped past him into the house. He stepped over the soiled shoes and around the shell crater, heard the door slam behind him, and headed off.

What happened was this: There was once an old woman, many years a widow, who spent her days sitting on her porch in a village called Plavno, watching the war pass around her. One afternoon as she rocked back and forth, bullets from a far hill poured into her house, sizzling and popping around her. She closed her eyes, and when the barrage was over she opened them again to find herself still among the living. This annoyed her greatly, for she had long since tired of the war, of the constant shortages of bread and wine, and was ready to take her place at the bountiful banquet table of the Lord.

The old woman clucked her tongue, stood, and hobbled into her house. In the kitchen, she found that some of the bullets had hit her dish cabinet; her best china was shattered, and she had no more glue.

From the kitchen she went to her bedroom, and found that a single bullet had struck the side of her armoire. She opened the armoire doors, and saw that the bullet had pierced her row of clothes. Each of her seven dresses now had one small hole in the chest, and she had no more thread.

From the bedroom she went to her bathroom, and there she found that her plumbing had also been hit. Water was pouring onto the floor, and she had no way of repairing the pipes.

The woman clucked her tongue again and set to work. She shut off the water valve and mopped the bathroom floor. She picked up the largest of the china fragments and saved them in a cardboard box on the mantle. The translucent slivers and glittering dust she swept out of her kitchen, through her living room, across her front porch and into the street. As for the dresses, well, they were her only clothes, so she continued to wear them, a different dress for each day of the week as she always had.

Shortly thereafter, a small dark spot appeared on her chest, directly beneath the bullet holes in her dresses. The spot grew darker with each passing day, and the woman assumed that this was because of the sunlight coming in through the holes. Then the spot began to bleed.

The old woman told her neighbors about this strange occurrence, the news quickly spread, and soon groups of strangers were showing up every day on her porch. They would ask to see the spot, and to touch it, and as they touched it they would cry thanksgiving to God for allowing them to witness such a miracle. The woman was very happy, because the visitors all brought bread and wine—one even brought tools and supplies with which to fix her bathroom pipes—and also because she had never been so popular before, as she was a churlish and greedy woman whose own children had left her as soon as they were able.

This continued for almost a month, but one evening a group of visitors knocked at the old woman's door, and there was no answer. They waited all night on her porch, afraid of waking her, and when they knocked again in the morning, once more there was no response. Fearing that some misfortune had overtaken her, they entered the house. They found her dead on the toilet.

The villagers came and washed the woman's body, placed her in bed, folded her arms across her chest, and kept a vigil for two days and two nights—they would have maintained it longer, but on the third day the body began to smell. The old woman was buried with all due ceremony in the town cemetery, and her house was rebuilt as a church: a cross was raised from the crown of the roof, and the punctured armoire was decorated as a shrine, with mirrors and bits of china, icons and candles and a statue of our Lord. The armoire-shrine was placed in the living room, where it stayed until it was stolen four days later by drunk soldiers who had abandoned their squad and needed money for boat tickets to Italy.

Part 2

5.

By early evening Joško's bread and potatoes were gone. He waited for nightfall, slipped into a vineyard, and filled his stomach with what fruit he could find. He thought of his own vines, hoped that his father was taking good care of them, wondered if the harvest had started on the coast.

The moon watched him from the horizon, and he could not return its stare. He refilled his canteen at a sluggish river, waded across, walked until he could see no lights in any direction, and curled beneath a tall cypress growing alone on a hillside.

He rose early the next morning, and stepped out from under the tree. The sun flooded his eyes, and he had trouble keeping his balance, but gradually his legs steadied. An hour, two hours, three, hill after hill, and the air began to change. It smelled more of stone and less of dust, more of clouds and less of rivers, and now it smelled of seawater.

He came to a dry crest, and before him was the Adriatic, alive and glowing. He dropped down the slope, crossed a wide road and walked to the water. He washed his hands and face, and the saltwater stung the wound in his head.

He dried himself with his bandana, straightened and looked around. To the northwest there was only the rock-studded coast. To the southeast, across a wide bay was the sharp white of a city he'd never seen before.

He kept to the shore, past refineries spitting yellow foam into the sea, past ships that rusted at anchor in the bay, and on the out-skirts of the city he found a bakery. As he entered, the woman behind the counter drew back.

- Excuse me, Joško said. Can you tell me where I am?

The woman looked at him as though he were rabid.

- This is Split.

- It is? I had no idea it was so beautiful.

The woman folded her arms and asked what he wanted. Joško thought for a moment. Once, when he was very young, his mother had made rolls covered with poppy seeds that a friend in Austria had sent her. Later he'd tried every bakery on the island and found noth-ing at all like the flavor of those rolls.

- Do you have anything with poppy seeds?

The woman shook her head.

- That's too bad. They're the most wonderful—

- Anything else?

- Plain rolls will be fine, I guess.

The woman walked to a bin at the far end of the counter.

- How many?

The bin was less than half full, and Joško asked for all of them. The woman filled two bags and part of a third, and tied the bags with twine.

- Will that be all?

- Yes, thank you.

Then he saw a small krempita. The sweet cream of its center spilled out through its flaky sides, and he asked for it as well. The woman wrapped it in waxed paper and put it on the counter beside the bread.

- Six thousand dinar.

Joško opened his rucksack, removed the envelope, and counted the money onto the counter. The bills were stiff with dried blood and rakija. The woman paled slightly.

- That's okay, she said. Consider it a gift for a brave soldier.

Joško smiled and thanked her. He made his way along the waterfront, eating the krempita as he went. All he needed now was some coffee, and then he'd find a bus headed south.

The sidewalks were full, men brandishing rolled newspapers like clubs, women clustered in front of window displays. He came to a wide street, and on one side was a bright cafe. He chose a table on the terrace, set his rucksack in one chair and sat down in another.

A jeep full of soldiers flew by, and he wondered how the war was going. Better than before, he hoped—would that be too much to ask? He decided he would corner the next soldier he saw, buy him a drink, get the latest news.

The cafe's only waitress ignored him for some time, and as she did, he remembered the joke he had thought of, and realized that now was the perfect time to play it. When she came to take his order he was ready, but his cheek was twitching so badly that he could barely talk. He scraped his cheek with a plastic ashtray until it quieted, and smiled at the waitress.

- I'd like two glasses of your best Dalmatian wine, he said. One for me and one for my friend here.

The waitress looked at him, at the empty chair across from him and the rucksack on the chair beside him.

- The war has been hard on you, hasn't it?

- Not really.

He tried to keep a straight face but didn't quite succeed, and the waitress mumbled something he didn't catch. She was back in a few minutes with the two glasses of wine, and set one down in front of him and the other in front of the empty chair.

- Not there. Didn't I say one for me and one for my friend?

Joško pointed to the placemat in front of the rucksack. The waitress shook her head, picked the glass up, put it where he had pointed. He opened his rucksack and rummaged through it until he found what he was looking for. He took it by the hair, pulled it out, and set it on the table in front of the glass.

- There you go, Hadžihafizbegović, he said. I've heard that you Muslims only drink coffee, but it's time you learned how to drink wine.

The waitress screamed and vomited and collapsed onto a nearby table. Joško looked at the head again. The eyes had glazed to an iridescent bluish-green. Blood had dried black around the mouth and nose, in streams from the hairy ears, in patches on what was left of the neck. The mouth was set in a tight grin.

A crowd was gathering, more and more people pushing forward to see, and their staring made Joško uncomfortable. Perhaps invisibility was better after all. He took his glass, tapped it on the table, lifted it to toast Hadžihafizbegović's health, and drank it down. He grabbed the head, then realized how silly it was to be carrying all that extra weight, and took out his knife. The murmuring grew louder around him. The joke had not worked at all, and he wondered what would have made it better.

6.

There was the smell of dust, and then of sweat, and then of hot metal. Joško opened his eyes and found himself lying in a bare vineyard.

It was late morning, and a line of ants was crawling along his outstretched arm. He brushed them off and opened his rucksack, felt a tickle on his neck, and noticed another line of ants leading from his shoulder to his shirt pocket. He flicked them away, and now he remembered: the cafe, the wine, the joke. A few young boys had followed him as he'd hurried out of the city. He had started to run, and by sunset he had been alone, and very, very tired.

He drew his knife, pulled out Hadžihafizbegović's ear and carved carefully around the earring, tucked it deep into his pocket, and hid the ear under a rock. He took a roll out of his rucksack and thought of the girl who had sung for him. She was beautiful, he was sure of it. As beautiful as Klara, maybe. He chewed the roll, and the girl was Klara and then she was not, and Klara was sitting alone in her bedroom. Light streamed through the window and across her face. She was thinking of him and hoping he was safe, but now the Serb ships started firing, there was the scream of a shell as it burrowed down through the air and Joško grabbed his things and ran.

He was barely out of the vineyard when his cheek started to twitch. He slowed to a walk, and a strange dizziness crept up from his stomach. His walking became a stumbling. Trees appeared from nowhere to block his path, and sweat ran from the tips of his fingers.

Images started flowing through his head, and the flow grew thick as sewage. There were unfamiliar faces that twisted together, cursing and then becoming each other, and now the images were only colors, browns and grays and shades whose names he didn't know. Joško fell, made it back to his feet, fell again and heard the rush of running water. He crawled blindly toward the sound, felt the soil go soft and damp, pulled himself forward and dropped face down.

✻

- Magarac! a voice shouted. Get over here!

Joško shuddered, turned, saw a burled brown arm. A moment later a bearded face appeared.

- Jesus, the mouth said. What a mess.

The face moved through and beyond Joško's sight, and he was lifted and carried, dropped in the back seat of a jeep, and he wept without understanding why.

- Handcuff him? Magarac asked as he settled in the passenger's seat.

- You can if you want, but I wouldn't bother.

The driver started the jeep and pulled onto the road. Magarac took a headset from the dashboard and lifted a microphone from between the seats. At first he said nothing but numbers, and his ears flared lightly as he spoke.

After a short silence he said, Not yet. Probably threw his tags into the sea the first chance he got.

Joško sat up, waited for his head to clear, and said, Where are we going?

The driver flinched and the jeep swerved and straightened. Joško looked back and forth between the two soldiers. They looked at him, then at each other.

- So you wouldn't bother, Magarac said.

The driver shrugged, and the jeep slowed down.

- My sister needs me, Joško said. I have to—

Magarac took a pair of handcuffs from his belt, turned in his seat, and now Joško knew. He lunged forward, shoved Magarac in the chest, watched as he pitched out of the jeep.

36

The driver swore, and the jeep skidded to a stop. Joško reached for the man's neck but he twisted easily free, turned and drove his fist into Joško's stomach. Joško curled up, trying to disappear into himself. The man punched him in the kidneys and spine, and Joško twitched and rolled as the pain swept his mind away.

＊

He woke again as the jeep pulled through a gate in a tall barbwire fence. A white line of barracks slid past. Joško's hands were cuffed behind his back, and his abdomen rippled with cramps.

The driver stopped in front of a squat gray building, got out and pulled Joško from the jeep, but his legs failed and he fell into the dust. The driver kicked him hard in the side and pulled him back to his feet. Magarac stood silently, holding his right arm to his chest, his nose scraped raw, blood running from a cut on his forehead.

Two guards came walking out of the building. One took Joško's rifle and rucksack, and the other led him toward the door. In the lobby was a clerk sitting behind a metal desk. As Joško came forward he took a clipboard out of the top drawer.

- Name and rank?

Joško didn't answer, and the clerk looked at Magarac.

- No idea. We found him passed out near a stream maybe twenty kilometers from here, and on the way back he attacked us and tried to escape.

- Okay. You want me to have the medic take a look at him?

- Nope. I like him just the way he is.

- Good enough, said the clerk. Take him to 12.

Joško was pulled down a hallway and around a corner. One of the guards took a ring of keys from his belt, opened the door to a storeroom and set Joško's belongings against the far wall. He closed the door, locked it, and walked on ahead as the other guard pulled Joško farther down the hall to a line of cells.

Here the air was slightly cooler. Each cell held three men, most of them in filthy army uniforms. Some slept, and others paced or prayed or cackled. One of the cacklers, a short fat man with a thick moustache and tiny eyes, reached out at Joško as he walked past. The guard kicked at the prisoner's hand, the fat man shrieked, and laughter echoed through the cellblock.

Cell 12 held only one prisoner, a gaunt pale man sitting in a pool of urine in the middle of the floor. Dried spittle crusted his beard, and when he saw Joško he rolled onto his stomach and scuttled into the farthest corner.

- Welcome to the Split Sheraton, said the guard who was holding Joško as the other opened the cell door.

Magarac stepped forward.

- Hold on a second.

The guard smiled, removed Joško's handcuffs, and Magarac kicked high into Joško's chest. Joško flailed and fell, landing in the pool of urine. The door slammed shut and the men walked away.

He dragged himself to the nearest of the three beds, rested for a moment before heaving himself up, but couldn't get his leg to catch on the mattress, and fell back to the floor. Under the bed was a small plastic pail, and Joško wondered who had left it there. He folded one arm under his head, and darkness lowered and held him.

✼

Joško felt someone pulling him onto his side, felt hands groping at his belt clasp. It was his cellmate, naked on the floor beside him. Joško shoved him away, cinched his belt and stood.

The man crawled to his bunk, got in and closed his eyes. Joško sat down and kneaded his stomach. Everything hurt, but his breath came easier, and the bed was at least as comfortable as his cot in Šibenik had been. There was a barred window set high in one wall, and he stared at the rectangle of sunlight that lay flat against the opposite wall. It stretched diagonally at one end, almost like the prow of a ship, and Joško remembered Klara, the Serb ships, the shelling.

He shouted for the guards, and the cellblock became a hoarse fanatic choir. A guard came running down the line of cells, swinging his baton to both sides, and walked slowly back up to Joško's cell.

- Did you start all this?

- I'm sorry, Joško said, but I have to go. My sister—

- You'll leave when the guys in 105 say you can leave. Until then, shut the fuck up or I'll break your elbows.

The guard walked up the hall and turned the corner, and Joško sat down on his bed. He listened to his cellmate crying in his sleep, and to the ranting of those in other cells. The rectangle of sunlight slid up to the center of the wall, widened into a perfect square and faded to nothing.

Then he heard footsteps. The two guards were escorting a battered soldier down the hall. One guard opened the door to Joško's cell, and the other thrust the soldier inside. The man's left hand was wrapped in blood-soaked bandages. He sat down on the one empty bed, swung his legs up and lay back.

- What happened to you? Joško asked.

The soldier looked across at Joško, and rolled over to face the wall.

The guards brought breakfast early the next morning: paper plates of bread and canned meat, paper cups of water. Joško took his plate and cup from the floor, went to his bed and emptied the cup in one long draught. His cellmates hadn't gone to get their food. The man who'd been there when he arrived was still asleep; the other soldier was sitting upright on his bed, and his eyes were open and empty.

- You really should eat something, Joško said.

- Why?

Joško had no answer. The man looked down at his bloody hand.

- What happened was, I didn't want to die.

- What?

The man scratched lightly around the bandages.

- I ran. We all ran, at least at the beginning. Some of us stopped, and some of us didn't. Me, for example. And Tomislav. And Dubravko.

- Where are they?

- I don't know. They were here a few days ago, but I don't think they'll be coming back.

- I don't understand.

The man stared at Joško.

- Deserters get taken to Room 105. Sooner or later you sign your confession and then you disappear.

- But if you're a deserter too—

- I told them that the others had forced me to go along because I was the only one who knew the trail. It wasn't a very good lie, but it was all I could think of.

- So they aren't going to take you away?

- Yes, they are.

- But if you didn't—

- I admitted everything yesterday.

- Why?

The soldier closed his eyes and folded his arms across his chest.

- You'll find out when they take you to 105.

7.

*T*he man with the injured hand was named Kunić, and the other man was named Gusterica. Gusterica lay on his bed and refused to eat, so Joško and Kunić split his food and water. Again Joško watched the skewed rectangle slide up the wall, become a square, and fade.

There were more shouts, a shriek, more footsteps, and standing at the door were Magarac and the two guards. Kunić backed into the corner of the cell. Gusterica didn't even open his eyes.

A guard opened the door, and Magarac stepped inside. His right arm was in a cast, and there were fresh white bandages on his nose and forehead. He told Joško to stand in the center of the cell, and not to move. Joško did as he was told, and Magarac nodded.

- Now you're going to tell me your name, your rank, and what you were doing by that stream instead of fighting the Serbs with the rest of your squad.

- My name is Joško.

- Joško what?

- Joško Banović.

Magarac smiled, then laughed, a tremendous braying that echoed down the cellblock.

- Ah. So you're the famous Joško Banović, the man who shot down two jets over Šibenik, who left the head of that Muslim sniper on a cafe table in Split.

Joško thought about bringing out the earring as proof, but of course if he did the guards would take it.

- I'm not sure it was Hadžihafizbegović, but—
- Brother, I'm going to give you one more chance. Who are you?
- Joško Banović.
- Of course you are. And I'm Marshall Tito.

Magarac smiled again, and drove his cast into Joško's groin.

- Let's try something else. Why don't you tell me why you deserted your squad.

Joško tried to answer, but no words came out.

- There's no hurry. Consider your answer carefully.

- It was a special mission. The planes came and killed them all, and now my sister—

Magarac hurled him into the wall.

- Are you making fun of me?

- No, I know, but she—

The man smacked him into the wall again.

- You're aware, right, that the war isn't going very well? That whole towns are being slaughtered? And do you know why? Because cowards like you are abandoning their posts. Now tell me the truth, or so help me—

- I did. The—

Magarac threw him to the floor.

- Fuck you and your God both.

Joško rose to his knees and looked up.

- And may my God fuck you back.

Magarac began kicking him, his boots thudding into Joško's stomach and chest. Joško clawed his way under the bed, and the two guards stepped in and pulled Magarac back to the door.

- I'll see you in Room 105, he said.

He wiped the sweat from his chin, and looked over at Kunić still huddled in the corner.

- And you'll be seeing me early tomorrow morning.

When the men were gone, Kunić came to Joško, helped him up and onto his bed.

- Your head's a mess.

- Yes.

- Seriously. You need to get it looked at.

- I know. Thanks.

Kunić hesitated.

- Are you really Joško Banović?

- Yes.

- Wow. I heard the guards talking about you yesterday—you were in the newspapers and everything.

Joško didn't reply. For a time Kunić stared at his bandaged hand. Then he walked to the corner of the cell, knelt on the floor, and rocked gently back and forth.

Joško didn't sleep much that night. Kunić stayed in the corner working through the rosary prayers, and Gusterica came over twice to fiddle with Joško's belt clasp. At last a thin light slipped in through the window. The guards came walking down the hall. One of them opened the door to the cell and drew his pistol. The other lifted Kunić to his feet.

❋

Magarac stopped by that evening to tell Joško that he had until the end of the week to think about what it meant to desert his squad, to betray the Motherland, to be a coward. Kunić did not come back, and no new prisoners were brought in. Gusterica still would not eat, so Joško ate for him, and the food seemed to be repairing what Magarac had broken.

For three days he saved his waste in the pail beneath his bed. After breakfast on the fourth day he went over to check on his cellmate. Gusterica was asleep, his eyelids scaly with dried pus and tears. Joško stepped to the door of the cell and called for the guards.

Again the other prisoners joined in the shouting, and again one of the guards came running down the hall, swinging his baton like a sword. Joško waved him to a stop.

- Gusterica hasn't been eating his food, and now I can't wake him up. I think he's dead.

The guard looked at Joško, then over at Gusterica.

- Shit. Okay. Go sit on your bunk, facing the wall. If you move at all, I swear to God I'll put a bullet in your brain.

43

The guard unlocked the door, stepped into the cell and closed the door behind him. He walked over to Gusterica and put his hand to the man's wrist.

- You asshole, he said, turning back around. He's—

Joško slung the contents of the pail into the guard's face and clutched at the man's throat. The two of them fell to the floor, rolling in the stew of feces and urine, and the guard lost consciousness before he could get his pistol out of its holster. Joško kept his grip on the man's throat a moment longer.

Now Gusterica's eyes were open wide. He stared at Joško, and his mouth moved but no sound came out. Joško nodded, took the key ring from the guard's belt and opened the cell door.

- Goodbye, Gusterica, he said. Best of luck.

His cellmate shook his head and started clawing at his mattress. Joško walked up the hallway, and all around him the prayers and ranting went quiet. One fat hand reached out to grab at his shirt. Joško stopped, looked at the prisoner, and the man drew his hand back in.

He found the storeroom, got the door open, took up his rifle and rucksack, turned around and met the second guard coming in. He drove the barrel of his rifle into the man's stomach. As the guard fell, Joško flipped the rifle around and swung it down again and again until the man's skull broke open.

Up the next hallway, into the lobby, and the clerk was standing in the far doorway, staring out at the morning. Joško brought his rifle back over his shoulder, drove the butt against the back of the man's neck and watched him fall.

Across the compound a group of guards stood talking and smoking, and to his right Joško heard the rumble of an engine. He walked around the corner, saw a jeep with its hood gaping open, and a soldier leaning in so far that one of his feet was raised off the ground. Joško stepped forward. It was Magarac. Joško watched the man work, then reached up for the hood and slammed it down.

The engine coughed thickly and Magarac's legs lifted, collapsing against the fender as the engine died. Joško opened the hood and pulled the body out. The fan had caught Magarac on the temple and peeled his face away.

- I'm sorry, Joško said.

The corpse did not answer. Joško dragged it over to the side of the building and stretched it out flat, taking care to fold one of Magarac's arms gently under his head. He put his rifle and rucksack in the back of the jeep and climbed into the driver's seat, turned the ignition key, and the engine spat and went silent. He turned the key again, and this time the engine hacked and sputtered, then roared.

Through the middle of the compound, past the circle of guards. The sentry shaded his eyes to get a better look. Joško took up his rifle, shot him in the chest, burst through the gate and out onto the road.

❋

The wind sang around him, and Joško smiled as he thought of how soon he would be at his sister's house. He reached back and pawed through his rucksack until he found what was left of the rolls he'd bought in Split. Ants had been at work on most of them, but at the bottom of the third bag he found several rolls that were still in fair shape. He pulled two of them out, and imagined his arrival in Dubrovnik: the gunboats were silent, and Klara was on her balcony, saw him walking toward her, came running down the stairs to embrace him.

The landscape went pale and dry as he flew along the ragged coast, slipping onto side roads when he could, shunting back down to the highway when there was no other choice. Hard bright cliffs grew from nothing to his left, and the sea mumbled and tossed to his right. He wondered if the spearfishing was any good here. Then the cliffs fell away, and a small village stretched along both sides of the road. He slowed when he saw children playing in a patch of sand nearby.

He counted the rolls he had left, checked his canteen and found it empty. He searched the sides of the road, and when he saw a stand with a sign advertising ripe tangerines, he pulled onto the shoulder and smiled at the pudgy woman who sat inside.

- Hello, he called. Is there somewhere around here where I could fill my canteen?

- Nothing is free, the woman said.

- And if I bought something first?

The woman shrugged, and scratched at the bristly black hairs that grew from the mole on her chin. Joško opened his rucksack, then saw a five-thousand-dinar note stuffed into a plastic box between the seats. He took the bill and held it out.

- What will this buy?

- Twenty figs, ten tangerines, or two melons.

Joško walked to the stand. The tangerines and figs looked good, but the melons were overripe, and some of them had started to rot. One was exactly the size of Hadžihafizbegović's head, and near the base there was a crack that curled up to either side like a grin, as if the melon, at least, had gotten the joke.

- Ten figs and five tangerines, please.

The woman reached under the counter and came up with a plastic bag. She blew it open, counted the figs into it, took up four tangerines and dropped them in as well.

- You—

- Minus one for the water, the woman said. You want free water, go to the sea.

- Where's the faucet?

The woman jerked her thumb around the corner of the stand, then covered her mouth and nose with her hand.

- You really stink, she said.

She took a closer look at his clothes, reached up and drew a heavy metal grate down between them. Joško found the spigot and filled his canteen. He washed his hands and face, his neck, his arms, and sprayed off his uniform as well as he could. As he walked back to the jeep he called his thanks to the grate. There was no reply.

A few kilometers farther on he came to a checkpoint, and it seemed that the soldiers were waiting for him. One stood in the middle of the road and signaled for him to stop. Another took out a clipboard, walked around behind the jeep, and shouted to the one in front.

Joško hunched as low as he could, slipped the gearshift into reverse and jammed the gas pedal to the floorboard. He felt the jolt of the soldier's body, put the jeep in first and hit the gas again. A bullet shattered the windshield, and there was another jolt, a soldier flying up over the hood, catching on the top of the windshield and again on the tailgate, tumbling away. Other soldiers along the road began firing, and then Joško was past them, past a row of tents that hunched like khaki vultures, and now he was alone with the sea and its pinpointed light.

There would be other checkpoints soon, he knew. He tried the first side road he came to, but it dead-ended only a few hundred meters inland. He tried the next one as well, and it curled southwest and burrowed into the hills.

What happened was this: There was once an old man, a vintner, who lived outside the village of Kopačevo, midway between Osijek and the Serbian border. He had worked as hard as he could his entire life producing the finest wines in the region, and as a result he had always lived comfortably. His cupboards were well-stocked with fresh vegetables, his bins with flour and sugar and salt, and his coop with a flurry of fat hens. He had a brilliantly colored rooster the size of a goose, two sheep, and a cow who provided him with three liters of the richest milk every morning.

However, as the war passed through the region, fewer and fewer people were able to afford the old man's wines. This did not worry him greatly, for he knew that sooner or later the war would end. He began to live frugally, eating at first two meals per day, and then only one.

When his money was gone, he began slaughtering his chickens, and they lasted him nearly a month. He killed the rooster as well, but the meat was so tough that he had to stew it for days on end. Now it was time to butcher his sheep, and he was not looking forward to the musky taste of their meat, but it turned out he needn't have worried. On the morning he went to herd them in, one of them stepped on a landmine, and the following evening the carcass of the other was stolen from where it hung in his barn.

Thus, with winter coming on, the vintner was forced to slaughter his cow. He begged her forgiveness as he sank the blade of his ax into her skull. In recent months he'd had little with which to feed her, and as he butchered her he saw that now she had equally little with which to feed him: her haunches were veined and spare.

48

As if such troubles were not enough, a few weeks later the old man's well, which for six generations had provided his family with clear cold water, suddenly went dry. Again and again he sent down the wooden bucket, and again and again it came up empty. For the first time in his life he became afraid.

The next day, he searched through his kitchen for something, anything, the smallest scrap to eat. He checked his pantry, his bins and cupboards. Finally he realized that he had nothing left.

Nothing, that is, but a cellar full of wine, a bottle from each of his many good vintages. He walked down the wooden staircase into the cool dry darkness, turned on the light, took the bottles in hand one after another, and tears slipped silently from his eyes.

As his Croatian neighbors had long since refused to pay what his wines were worth, he had no choice but to cross the border into Serbia. He chose eight of his very best bottles, placed them in his leather knapsack, took up his walking stick and set off.

It was a four-hour walk to the border, and another three hours to the village of Sonta. By the time he arrived the sun had set. His burden was not light, and he was very tired, but he knew that he could not rest. He made his way to the threshold of the most brightly lit house in town. There he knocked, and awaited his fate.

The man who opened the door was none other than the mayor himself. Gathered in his living room were the village's wealthiest inhabitants, merchants who came each night to drink the mayor's brandy and talk of better times.

'Come in, come in,' said the mayor. 'There is always room for one more by my fire. Take a seat here with us, and tell us your story.'

The vintner sat down, and lowered his knapsack to the polished floor. He accepted a glass from his host, drank deeply, and said, 'I come from Kopačevo, across the border.'

The room went silent, or nearly so; only the fire spoke, hissing words of warning. The vintner hesitated, then added, 'You must believe that you have nothing to fear from me. I am simply an old man with nowhere else to go.'

The merchants began to protest, but the mayor silenced them. 'Sir,' he said, 'this is my home, and you are my guest. No harm will come to you here.'

The old man took another sip of brandy. 'I have worked as hard as any man alive,' he said, 'to ensure that in my latter years I would live without worry. But the war has taken everything from me. My cupboards are empty. I have slaughtered my chickens, and even my milk cow. My well is dry. All I have left are the best of the wines I have made. I had hoped to savor them with old friends, and know that in the course of my life I'd brought something of value into the world. I offer them to you now in the more modest hope that you will pay a fair price, so that I might survive the coming winter and live to harvest again next year.'

The old man opened his knapsack and took out the eight bottles of wine. One by one he set them on the floor, turning them so that the labels could be read by all in the room.

The wealthy men of Sonta began talking excitedly among themselves, trying to guess the prices the old man would ask, and the extent to which they could bargain him down. But at a word from the mayor they fell quiet. He sent for food to be brought, and as his servant carried in boards of bread and cheese and roasted meat, the mayor drew out a leather purse that was already half full of bills. He made his way around the room, and from each of the gathered merchants he asked as much as could be spared.

The men grumbled at first, but in the end each gave generously, and by the time the mayor returned to the vintner, the leather purse was nearly bursting. 'Keep your good wines,' he said. 'Take this for now, harvest well in the coming year, and may you repay us as soon as God and good fortune allow.'

So moved was the old man by their generosity that he cried, 'Then let what I have brought be my gift to all of you!' A corkscrew was called for, the bottles were opened one by one, and the merchants marveled at the color and clarity and flavor of each of the eight wines. When the last bottle was empty, more brandy was brought, and the men talked long into the night of the blessings that God granted even in these hardest of times.

As the fire died and morning began to glow in the windows, the others took their leave, and the mayor showed the old man to the finest of his guest rooms. In the deep feather bed the vintner slept as soundly as he ever had. In fact, he slept well into the following day. When he awoke and saw the afternoon light filtering through the trees outside, he dressed quickly and hurried into the living room. A satchel of bread and cheese and sausage was waiting beside the door, along with his knapsack, his walking stick, and the leather purse.

The mayor came out of his kitchen with a smile on his face. Much embarrassed, the old man apologized for being such a poor guest. 'Don't even speak of such things,' said the mayor, as the servant brought a tray of coffee and rolls into the room. 'You were very tired, and sleep is the only cure for such a sickness.'

The two of them ate and drank in comfortable silence. At last it was time for the old man to go. He embraced his host warmly and thanked him for all that he'd done, and the mayor wished him the most pleasant of journeys home.

The old man walked steadily as the afternoon faded into evening, stopping only when he reached the border. There, just before crossing over, he ate of the food the mayor had given him.

Hours later, as he picked his way through the final stretch of woods near his home, he noticed a strange reddish light playing off the clouded sky above him. Then he smelled smoke, and suddenly branches were breaking all around him. Flashlight beams scurled at his feet and up to his face, and a pack of Serb soldiers was upon him.

The old man was knocked to the ground, and the contents of his knapsack spilled onto the path. One of the soldiers snatched up the purse, and another the satchel of food. The others kicked the old man about the head and chest until he lay gasping and bloody on the trail.

The captain of the squad took pity on him, and commanded his men to stop the beating. 'Wine!' he shouted. 'A sip of wine for the poor bastard!'

All of the soldiers laughed at this, and one of them brought a bottle to the old man's lips. Though most of the wine spilled down his chest, the taste was oddly familiar.

'Please,' he sputtered, 'please tell me, where did you get that wine?'

'From the cellar of a house not far from here,' said the captain. 'We took all the bottles we could carry, and shattered the rest.'

'But... but it is wine from my own cellar!' said the old man.

'If that's the case, you'd better hurry home! We torched your house, and even now your vineyards are burning.'

Part 3

8.

*E*arly light burnished the sides of the valley and glazed the branches of the olive tree under which Joško had spent the night. He fumbled through his rucksack until he found his canteen. As he drank the last of his water, he felt something snap and slip from around his neck. He lifted his shirt, and his abalone-shell necklace fell to the ground.

The broken leather thong was stiff and black with dried sweat. He tossed it into the grass, and polished the shell with his bandana. On the pearled inner surface he saw a reflection of the raw black outline of his eye, but upside down, elongated and strange. He rubbed the shell with his thumb and studied the reddish topside, its miniscule snags and cornices. He remembered a sea that had once been his, and other seas he'd studied in school. There were so many.

Dubrovnik was only a dozen kilometers away, due west back through the hills, and Klara would make him a new necklace. Joško tucked the shell into his rucksack and fixed himself breakfast, building something like sandwiches from his four tangerines and the stale rolls that remained. The tangerines had turned to mush in his rucksack, but at least the mush was sweet, and what juice remained was sufficient.

Below him he saw a glint off the windshield of the jeep that had carried him so far and so well before the motor finally gave out. He thought of the singing girl, and wondered if someone else had found her. Why else would she have stopped singing? Were the two of them living happily together even now? He struck himself on the forehead, and got to his feet.

He stayed on the road until he saw an army truck coming toward him, then waded into the brush and headed for the lowest pass he could see, threading himself up through sandstone ravines. The creeks that had formed them had long since gone dry; in the deeper depressions there were moist mud banks, but there was no water to drink. Black wasps circled and landed and rose up to follow him, clinging to the sides of his rucksack until he crushed them one by one with his open hand.

By midday his cheek was dancing furiously. Everything around him was heat and dust and bleached gray stone. He broke into the open again, his clothes weighted with sweat, and fought to keep his balance along the hillside trails.

At last he reached the crest, and below him was Dubrovnik: the famous city wall stood high and bright. On a nearby bluff was a radar dish flanked by anti-aircraft batteries, but the dish lay on its side, pointing nowhere. He made his way to the bottom of the hill and crossed the road. For a moment he rested in the dense shade of the wall, staring at what was left of an old tractor, its wheels gone and its body pierced and scarred.

He rounded the corner and walked through the gates into a steep alley that led down toward the center of the city. The cobblestones were slick with dust and age. He didn't know his sister's address, but in her letters she had mentioned that her house was on the north wall, that her one regret was that she couldn't see all the way to Jezera.

Soon he was standing at the midpoint of a wide avenue, and a sign on a nearby wall called it the Stradun. At one end was a high portal, and mounted above it was a bronze clock whose arms were figures of ancient gods. According to the clock it was a quarter after one. There was a church held together by scaffolding, with a clean round hole perhaps five meters wide in its roof, as though some tumor had been removed and the wound had not yet healed. To his left was a cluster of cafes, each with its radio playing a different song.

The city as a whole was less damaged than he had imagined. Masons and carpenters were at work on the ragged edges of the houses that had been hit. Shattered tile and splintered wood had been swept into piles in the corners of the courtyards. There were women with wet hands hanging sheets from clotheslines. From somewhere came the sound of a piano, the music filling and emptying like tide pools.

He passed a massive villa that was missing most of its windows. The balustrade on the upper courtyard had been broken in several places, and the wide terraced gardens were clotted with weeds. An empty fountain held a tall male nude, headless, and Joško could not tell if the damage was old or new.

On the far side of the villa he found a stairway leading up the north wall. At the top was a turret holding an ancient cannon. Far off, the sun was burning into the sea. Closer at hand was an island, barren on its right side and dark with cypress on its left. Below him was a group of people gathered on the rocky shore. Some of them slept, and others were playing cards. Children dove into the rigid blue.

There was no way out of the turret except back the way he had come, and once down he couldn't find any other staircases leading to the houses above. Then from a shuttered window a woman's voice called to him, demanding to know what he was doing on her patio.

- I'm looking for the house of Klara and Mislav Petan.

There was a long quietness, and one of the shutters opened. The woman appeared, a stained towel wrapped around her head.

- And who are you? she asked, her voice softer than before.

- I'm Klara's brother, Joško.

A fly buzzed at the hole in his head, and he brushed it away. The woman stared at him with an expression he did not understand.

- Take the alley to your right, she said. It leads straight to the bottom of their stairs.

The woman stepped back from the window and closed the shutter. Joško walked up the alley, and its paving stones were covered with fine white dust. He climbed the stairs to a terrace. The door leading into the house was ajar, and its trim was hanging loose.

He took three quick steps to the threshold, pushed the door open and saw what was left of the ceiling: a fringe of red slate, jagged as broken teeth, and beyond the wreckage a gutted moon hung from the sky. His legs gave out as he stepped into the room, and he staggered sideways, fell, landed hard on his side. He stared at the cracks in the walls. Too late, he thought. Too late.

A moment later he heard a noise behind him. Joško got to his knees. Standing on the terrace was a heavy-set man wearing a black fedora, pressed wool slacks, a perfectly white long-sleeved shirt.

- You are Klara's brother?
- Yes.
- I know how all this looks, the house and the roof, but Klara is fine. She and Mislav weren't getting on so well, I guess. She packed her things and left for your parents' house. That was the day before the shell hit.

Joško leaned back and smiled.

- I'm afraid Mislav wasn't so lucky.

Joško tried to look sad, and could tell that it wasn't working. The old man fanned himself with his hat, took a blue silk handkerchief out of his pocket, wiped the sweat from his forehead and looked at Joško carefully.

- Are you going to be all right?

Joško nodded. The man folded his handkerchief and replaced it in his pocket. Joško closed his eyes and listened to the footsteps echoing down the stairs. He had his next mission, but everything was so far away.

9.

The walls seemed to shudder. Joško looked around, but everything was still. Sweat dribbled from his hands and face, and he stood unsteadily, fell, stood again, and the room rushed around him.

His rucksack had overturned and its contents were scattered among the remains of the house. He grabbed at his canteen and found it empty, stumbled to the kitchen sink and turned on the tap. Nothing came out. He fell and could not stand, crawled to the bathroom, clutched at the basin, and nothing came out there either but there was water in the toilet, and he cupped his hands and drank.

The walls rippled and cracked, tiles dropped from the fringe of roof overhead and shattered on the floor around him, plaster rained down and now Joško understood. He hurried to the living room and started gathering his things. A third shell exploded, and he jumped to the open door, down into the courtyard and up the street, and others were running with and against him, pushing and screaming toward somewhere safer.

He fought his way down an alley, falling and catching himself and running again, out into a wide avenue. The cafe lights shut off one after another around him, and the avenue was a lake of sharp white music going gray. Up a cobbled street, a fourth explosion, a fifth so close that it threw him to the ground, and he landed on a middle-aged woman. She was dead but her eyes were open. Joško got to his feet, knelt back down to close her eyes, looked up at the massive bronze clock above the portal, and according to the clock it was still a quarter after one.

He took off running again, up a long narrow street and out the city gates. A jeep clipped his rucksack and spun him around. He righted himself and ran up the hillside until he was gasping and staggering and could not run any more.

Step by step, he climbed through the dusk to the ridgeline. He stumbled across it, slid a few meters down the far side, and came to rest. He set down his rifle and lay back. The silence grew thick and slow and wide.

He started walking, and the noise of his footsteps chipped holes in the night. His thirst tightened and rose in his throat, and heat flared in his chest, in his head. The hill steepened and turned to shale and Joško was falling, down the escarpment and into a gully, and there was no water but his hands landed in cool mud. He rubbed the mud onto his face, onto his neck and arms and chest. It was not enough and there was nothing else.

❋

By dawn, all he could think of was water. He stopped to dig through his rucksack and of course his canteen was empty but he found a bag of figs, all of them smashed and dry. He scraped a mouthful of reedy pulp from the bag, and had to spit it out to keep from choking. He tried again, and this time he was able to swallow.

When the pulp was gone he tried to remember how far it was to the last village he had seen on his way to Dubrovnik—two kilometers at least, maybe more. He got to his feet and started north along the ridge, afraid of falling, afraid of what might happen if he stopped. He walked, and the horizon began to swell with light. An hour, another. The sun stretched into the sky. He walked, and the heat settled like wool on his shoulders.

Then his legs seized and faltered, and he fell. He stared at his legs, willing them to lift him. They did not. Wondering if this was the place the world had chosen for him to die, he looked out over the flatlands below. Against the sun's glare he saw the far low shadows of buildings.

The shadows lightened and disappeared, took form and reached for him, disappeared again as he stumbled forward. Abruptly he was there, on the outskirts of a dusty village. Beside an empty corral he found a spring surrounded by agave with spines as long as fingers. He knelt and brought the clear sweet water to his mouth, but his throat closed in on itself, would not let the water pass. On his third try, a slight trickle found its way down. Another trickle, another, his throat opened and he was drinking freely, as fast as he could.

He filled his canteen and stood up. It was time to find his way back to Jezera. He would tell his stories at school, would be visible now, would be known. Klara was waiting, and the two of them would walk the tide pools together again. He would find shells for her, the most beautiful shells she had ever seen.

He took a step, and the spines of the tallest agave caught at his shirt. He pulled, and the agave held him; he jerked away, and his shirt tore. Holding the two tattered edges, he felt no longer whole. He searched through his things and found a small plastic bag that held a needle tucked into a spool of white thread. He pulled the needle out and attempted to thread it, but could not see the needle's eye. He took a deep breath, tried to focus on the tiny hole, but his hands were trembling, everything blurred and spun, he dropped the needle and fell to the ground.

For a time there was nothing in his mind but flecks of brown and white that moved like iron filings drawn by a magnet. The flecks were on the verge of forming a pattern, of showing him something, when the magnetic field collapsed and the flecks scattered and swirled, a tiny sandstorm, and he was nothing inside of it. He could not remember what he had been doing, could not remember anything he had ever done, was certain only that none of it mattered, that nothing he could do would make it matter.

Then sifting through the sandstorm was a noise. Joško opened his eyes, and the world spread out away from him, and the noise became a song. He did not understand the words, but it was the voice of the girl, and it was coming from far to the north.

For a crippled moment he considered ignoring her altogether. He already had a mission. The girl had abandoned him once, and might do so again. But her voice rose in pitch and volume, rose until the sound was more a scream than a song, and Joško knew there wasn't much time.

What happened was this: There was once an old woman, many years a widow, who lived—

I know. But this is a different story. Just listen.

There was once an old woman, many years a widow, who lived in a village called Otok, east of Sinj. She was a good-hearted person, and the war made her feel, more than anything, very, very sad—sad for the dead of her country, and for the dead of those who attacked her country. She was one of those rare spirits who feel all the pain in the world, and choose to go on living anyway.

She did what she could for everyone around her, baking loaves of bread with flour she could not spare, and leaving them on the porches of the houses whose doors bore the black ribbons that speak of death. Then one afternoon as she was returning home, artillery shells began to fall, and as she opened her front door there was an explosion that threw the old woman off her feet.

'My!' she thought. 'That was close!' She got up, straightened her clothes, went into her house... and found that it had no roof. The shell had struck her very home.

Late that evening the enemy was driven back and Otok was saved. And strange though it might sound, the old woman learned to be thankful for the shell that had taken away her roof. In the daytime, sunlight poured through the hole and warmed her face, and at night she could see the stars and hear them singing, precisely as God intended.

Then the winter came.

Part 4

10.

Joško spent the night curled up in a bare vineyard outside another dust-sotted village. At sunrise a woman came out of the house, walked to where he lay, stood over him. He told her that everything was okay, that he had a vineyard too, and had always taken good care of it. The woman said nothing. He got to his feet, brushed the soil from his clothes and gathered his belongings.

He climbed a low promontory, and below him was a road and a wide, sullen river. Fifty meters away both the river and the road swept to the north. He stumbled down the incline and across the road to the riverbank, and followed the water upstream.

Whenever he heard a car coming he hid in the reeds that grew tall and full along the bank. Kilometer after kilometer, and through all of it, the viscous time and heat, his cheek fluttered like the broken wing of a small bird. He listened to the voice of the girl, and her singing grew distant at times, fading altogether now and then. Each time it faded he entreated it to come back, and sooner or later it always did.

The lowlands rose into hills, and an hour later he was deep in the cleft of a valley. Here the river was brown with rancid mud, but the sun was raging overhead; he knelt in the shallows and drank until nausea welled up from his stomach and singed the back of his throat.

He stood and looked at the bluffs to either side. They were so blue and beautiful he almost fell, and it had been so long since he'd eaten. He pushed on, the bank growing thinner and thinner until there was nowhere to walk. He picked his way along, jumping from boulder to boulder. Then a town of gray stone appeared above him.

He fought his way up from the bank, stretching from hand-hold to handhold. At last he crossed a path with shallow stairs cut into the side-hill. He followed the switchbacks until he reached a road that led into town.

The first person to see him was a fat young boy who sat on a bench spitting olive pits into his hand and sucking them back into his mouth. The boy squealed and gagged and ran toward his mother, who had emerged from a nearby house and stood hunchbacked and furious on the sidewalk.

Joško crossed to the far side of the street. All around him he heard doors slamming and curtains being drawn. He didn't understand why until he saw his reflection in a shop window: blood and mud and dried sweat, his torn shirt, his matted hair.

Farther up the street, overlooking the town square was a strange round church, and the spike of its minaret punctured the low sky. In the center of the square was a well, and he drew a bucket of water. He took out his bandana and washed his face and neck, scrubbed his hands and arms, took off his shirt and washed his chest and what he could reach of his back.

A small group of women gathered around him, and they were dressed in clothes Joško remembered having seen somewhere before—blouses that swirled with bright colors, loose pants tied with drawstrings. He put his shirt on and pushed his hair out of his eyes.

- I'm very hungry, he said to the one who stood closest. Do you know where I can get something to eat?

One by one the women walked away. Joško didn't blame them. He filled his canteen, rinsed out his bandana, picked up his rifle and rucksack and continued through the town. Most of the buildings were skeletons. Shattered roof tiles covered the ground like shale. In the center of the block was a large gray hotel, its façade a labyrinth of bullet holes.

Wooden shacks lined the sidewalk, and sitting inside them were old men selling postcards and trinkets. Light came through the holes in the roofs, and glittered around the heads of the old men.

Joško stopped at one of the shacks. The old man had one postcard left. It was a beautiful picture of a long white bridge arcing over a river of dense blue-greens. Joško took it and asked its price. The man said nothing. Joško thanked him and put the postcard in his rucksack.

In the middle of the next block he found a bakery. He wiped his boots on the mat and stepped inside. There was no one at the counter but the oven was lit. He stood and waited, and finally a tall white-haired woman came out from the back.

- Hello, Joško said.

The woman's eyes went from fear to hatred to disgust.

- What? she asked. You have taken everything, and still you want more?

Joško was too tired and hungry to explain that he had never been to the town before.

- Something to eat, he said. Anything.

He opened his rucksack and took out his envelope of blood-stained bills. The woman reached for the envelope, looked inside, and threw it into the oven behind her.

- You shell our village and kill our sons, and now you offer me money? What makes you think I would take money from you?

Joško watched his money burn, shook his head and opened his rucksack again. Inside he found the medal he'd been given in Šibenik. He took it out of its plastic case and squeezed it in his hand, tighter and tighter until he began to tremble. But of course he had no choice.

- Will you accept this?

The woman took it, looked at it carefully, and closed her eyes.

- Of what possible good is this to me?

- I don't know. Perhaps you could sell it, or give it to your children. Children like bright things.

She stared at him for a time, then handed the medal back.

- I have no more children, the woman said. But you can have three rolls. That is all I can spare.

- Do you have the kind with poppy seeds?

- No. They are all plain, but very fresh.

She picked three rolls out of a bin and placed them on the

counter. He thanked her, put them in his rucksack, went to the door and turned back. The woman was still watching him.

- After the war, he said, perhaps you will have other children.

- I am too old to have any more children.

- Yes, but I once heard about a woman who was ninety years old, and God came to her and gave her a child.

- That is nothing but an old story.

- It might still be true, though. Some stories are true, you know.

He smiled, and the woman slipped away from him into the back of the store.

❋

Joško followed the road through what remained of the town. A strip of shell-pocked pavement stretched down toward the river, and to one side he saw a thick white pillar. On the pillar was a plaque, and the symbols on the plaque were from an alphabet he had never seen.

Beyond the pillar was a bridge, or what had once been a bridge. There was a platform of dusty white stone leading into the air, but there it stopped, reaching into emptiness like the stub of someone's arm. Joško began to cry, quiet gasps at first, then sobs that wracked his body. The girl started singing, and this helped him to catch his breath, but her voice was again distant, and when the song ended he heard nothing more.

Thirty meters upstream, the river cut hard to the east: he would have to find some way across. He stepped past the ruined bridge and edged down a path worn into the bank. A bright span glimmered before him, but as he raised his eyes, his foot caught on a rock. He slid several meters on his chest, and stopped short against some sort of cold metal mesh.

It was the side of a footbridge. Joško got to his feet and climbed around to the entrance. The bridge rattled beneath him, its metal slats like ribs cleaned by ants. A sudden wind clawed at him, and he clutched at the mesh, held to it until the wind died.

On the far bank he headed up a deserted road that slipped through a pass in the hills, and here everything was different. The air was still very hot but he managed to stay mostly in the shade of the oaks that grew on the hillsides. Hours of this, and the sun slid into the horizon, and the girl's singing came back to him.

He stopped walking to listen more carefully. Her voice began to rise, grew louder and louder, became pure scream. He covered his ears but it did no good—the scream was inside him now. He begged it to quiet, and the scream stretched up and out and back deeper into him. He dropped to his knees and the scream was cut short.

Joško removed his hands from his ears. There was no sound but the thin buzz of wasps. He sat down in the dry grass. The sky faded toward darkness.

11.

Joško woke wrapped in a horrible silence. The sun was already well into the sky, and sweat was beaded on his face. He sat up, held his breath and closed his eyes. Even the insects had fallen quiet. So that was that. He'd failed. The girl was dead or taken.

He headed west, and the hills grew into mountains. He came to no villages and passed few roads. When his course led uphill his lungs tightened and strained, and when it led downhill his legs pulsed and flared, giving way every so often and pitching him from the path. Each time it was a little more difficult to get up.

As afternoon fell to dusk he climbed the last mountain he'd have strength for that day. He neared the ridge, hoping that on the far side he'd see nothing but flatlands. Instead there was another range of mountains.

He sat down in the pass, ate a roll, drank what was left of his water. If the mountains did not end soon he would never see Klara again. He had walked so far and found so little.

He heard the taut keen of a hawk somewhere above him, and the crescent moon hung close in the sky, dagger-sharp and deadly. He burrowed into the grass, hoping that the moon had not seen him, could not hear his quickening heart.

❈

Joško knew that if he didn't find a village soon he would have to follow the next road he came to and take his chances with jeeps and soldiers. He dropped into the valley and started up the next hill. An hour later the sun was up, and his throat closed in on itself once again.

He worked his way from tree to tree, pulling himself along with the help of low branches. Each footstep raised a small plume of dust. The trail led to a ravine, and he slid down into the bottom, clawed his way up the far side. He pounded his legs with the sides of his fists and waited for his lungs to cool, then pushed on, one cramped step after another.

The ridgeline was tremendously distant. When he couldn't walk any farther he stopped in the shade of a massive dark stone and closed his eyes. Jezera seemed unreachable, but that left him nowhere to go. Then something brushed against his arm. He opened his eyes, and standing beside him was a boy with dirt crusted around his mouth, and hair twisted like kelp down his back. The boy smiled at him, and Joško smiled back. He tried to say hello, but a harsh unfinished whisper was all that came out.

The boy pointed at the ridge. Joško nodded. The boy slipped his hand into Joško's, took a step forward and pulled. Joško lifted his right foot and planted it higher. The boy grinned, took another step, and pulled again.

Each step upward seemed a separate life, but the boy would not let him stop. The horizon began to drop in the sky. Joško leaned on the boy's shoulder, and limped the last few steps to the pass.

A wide flat valley stretched away from the foot of the mountains. Joško dropped his rucksack and knelt down, tried to thank the boy but no words would come. The boy brought his hand to his mouth, to his ear, and shook his head.

Joško opened his rucksack and worked through it. He found a postcard of a bridge, a sewing kit, a carton of cigarettes, and handed them all to the boy. The boy nodded his thanks, and pointed at the knife on Joško's belt. Joško pulled it out of its sheath. Old blood had dried black on the blade. He wiped it on his tattered shirt, turned it in his hand and held it out. It was immense in the boy's palm, and he smiled, tucked it into his waistband, and pointed down the hillside.

A hundred meters below was a small white house. The boy patted his chest, pointed south along the ridge and turned to go, but Joško caught him by the back of the shirt and motioned for him to wait. The boy nodded. Joško searched around for a stick, cleared away a patch of grass, and scratched 'Jezera?' into the dry soil. The boy shrugged. Joško smoothed the ground as best he could and wrote 'Murter?'

The boy stared at the word, looked up into the sky, and pointed down the valley. Joško rose, kissed the boy on the forehead and watched as he walked down the ridge, then headed toward the house.

He went onto his tiptoes to look in through the back window. Books and magazines were scattered across the kitchen table, and dirty dishes were stacked on the counter. He made his way down the side of the house, stepped carefully through the withered flower-beds, rounded the corner and stopped.

Sitting in a straight-backed chair on the front porch was a very old woman. She was watching the valley as if waiting for something to begin. On a small table beside her were the remains of her lunch: a bit of salad, a crust of bread, part of a potato dumpling and a glass of water.

He stepped forward and cleared his ravaged throat. The woman's head swung around. It took a moment for her eyes to focus, and when they did she chirred like a squirrel, pushed herself up from her chair and stuttered toward her door.

Joško had never seen such slow hurrying. She finally reached the threshold, hopped inside and closed the door, and still he waited. When it was clear that she wouldn't be coming back out, he stepped onto the porch and helped himself to what she'd left. The water first, and it was easier this time, the liquid slipping down and his stomach quickly cooling. Then a bite of potato dumpling, the bread-crust, a mouthful of salad, and the plate was empty.

He looked up to see the curtains drawing shut. So he wasn't welcome to what he'd had, nor welcome to ask for more. He found a well on the far side of the house, drew up a bucket of water and took a long draught, filled his canteen, and dropped down the final hill.

❋

From time to time he passed other houses, and from the few that were empty he stole what food he could find. He followed a creek so that water would not be a problem, and avoided roads as best he could, crossing only when he could see no one in either direction.

Dusk now thickened the sky. The creek emptied into a culvert too wide to jump across, but there was a makeshift bridge, two tree trunks laid side by side. Joško was sad to see the creek end. His eyes traced the layers of soil and stone, the alternating grays in its banks. His cheek twitched once and went still.

He walked onto the bridge, then heard voices, jumped down and hunched in the scrub. A pair of women passed by, complaining about the price of potatoes. He waited until they were gone, climbed back onto the bridge, and was halfway across when he saw someone step up on the far end. It was a young man about Joško's age. A leather patch covered his left eye, and aside from the patch he was wearing only his underwear.

The two men were now face to face, and the bridge was not wide enough for either to slide cleanly past. The man scratched his stomach, and motioned for Joško to step aside. Joško stared at the leather patch, and a dizziness took him, the patch faded in and out of focus, the glistening surface, he seemed to be slipping through it and then felt a blow to his chest as the man pushed past. Joško leaned away, out and over the edge of the bridge, spinning his arms to keep from falling.

❋

The following morning he heard artillery fire, distant but getting closer. The barrage grew more and more intense, the reverberations shivering up through his legs. He crossed to the far side of the valley, came to a wide road, and heard the low rumble of vehicles coming toward him. He jumped from the roadway and dove into a lavender thicket.

A pair of jeeps flew by, and then a convoy of trucks loaded with soldiers. The soldiers jolted against one another. Some had their eyes closed, the rest stared blankly at the landscape, and they all looked exhausted. Joško hoped the war was going well, wished only the best for these soldiers, then wondered why their uniforms were so different from his, why the insignias on the trucks—

The soldiers were Serbs. They'd gotten this far. And how much farther? Šibenik? Tribunj? Jezera?

For the next several hours he jogged when he could, walked when he had to, and kept the road in sight. He saw more jeeps and trucks, heard more artillery fire. His rucksack and rifle were immensely heavy on his shoulders. The horizon blurred and shifted. Hills rose in front of him, and faded when he tried to climb.

Night came, but he didn't stop until he saw the fluttering glow of a campfire. He watched for a while, then picked his way forward—his canteen was empty, he had nothing to eat, and maybe it wasn't soldiers, maybe it was only... But now he heard voices coming from around the flames, and he did not recognize the accent. A faint wind stirred the leaves around him, and Joško walked quietly away.

❀

The sun was not yet above the horizon but the sky was softly bright. Joško skirted a high rock bluff, heard the thick hush of water, and then another sound, a hum that was almost familiar.

He came out of a dense stand of pines, felt the sun now on his back, and his shadow stretched long and loose and strange along the path. He looked down a grassy hill and across a maze of blackberry bushes. Beyond was a shallow river, and to his right was a concrete dam.

Two hundred meters downstream there was a small village, but no people were in sight. Joško sat on the hilltop to rest. A breeze rose from the river, poured over him, and he heard a girl's voice.

He jumped to his feet, scanned down the hillside and saw her kneeling on the near side of the river, washing clothes in the diamond-blue water. She was wearing a streaming white dress, a black apron, a black handkerchief over her head. The breeze softened, and now he could barely hear her, but it was her true voice, at last her true voice.

Then the humming from the dam went silent. Nothing else seemed to have changed, and it was so much easier to hear the girl singing. The colors slipped through her hands, crimson and emerald and rich royal blue. He stood and watched, closed his eyes and listened, opened his eyes, and four men crept out of the bushes behind her.

The men were oddly dressed—almost like janitors, Joško thought, with their coveralls and boots. Then he saw their weapons, and he dropped his rucksack and threw himself down the hill. He lost sight of the girl as he entered the blackberry thicket, but now he heard her scream, and he fought through the vines that caught and strained to keep him, the thorns that tore at his hands and face.

The maze thinned as he neared the water, and the girl's screams were cut off. He went to his hands and knees, crawled forward a few meters more, and parted the lower vines of the last bush between him and the riverbank.

One of the men had drawn the girl over a large stone in the river. Her dress was pulled up and over her head, and another man had mounted her from behind, his buttocks thrusting white in the sun.

Joško raised his rifle, took a deep breath, released it, took another, let it halfway out and put a bullet through the temple of the man who was holding the girl. The two men who had been watching and laughing lifted their guns. Joško shot them both, the right and then the left, and they too fell away.

The fourth man pulled back from the girl and turned toward the bank. Joško waited. The man brought his hands down to cover his dark groin. Joško shot him in the face, and he twisted and fell, threshing the water. Joško came to the edge and watched until the man's body went still.

The girl stared at Joško, blood running down her throat from a cut on her chin, her eyes sick with fear. He reached out his hand. The girl didn't move. Joško thought for a moment, unbuttoned his pocket, pulled out the earring and held it up for her to see. The girl stepped forward, then screamed and ran flailing toward the village.

Joško looked at the earring. There was still a bit of earlobe attached, and a little dried blood. He put it back in his pocket and went to follow her, but slipped and fell headlong, the barrel of his rifle plunging into the mud. He righted himself, and by now she was well ahead of him. He ran faster and faster and wasn't far behind when she entered the village and turned down an alley.

He got to the corner in time to see the muddy tails of her dress disappear through a doorway, and the door slam shut behind her. He reached the door, wiped the mud from his face, and went to knock.

The door swung open, and an old man with an ax was coming toward him. Joško stepped back and raised his rifle. The man did not stop and Joško squeezed the trigger, the bullet seized in the mud-filled barrel and the gun exploded. Pain ripped through Joško's hands and his right eye went dark.

He stumbled backwards, fell, got to his feet as the old man swung and the ax ripped through the cloth of his shirt. The man stepped forward and Joško turned and jumped; the man shouted, and doors up and down the alley began to open. Other men now, other hands grasping at Joško as he ran. He reached the street and saw the river on the far side, heard footsteps behind him, ran to the bank and hurled himself into the water, thrashing and then swimming as the river deepened, kicking away from the singing ax.

Joško swam on and on, turned to look back, and the old man was still standing on the bank, howling with anger and swinging his ax back and forth, but the world had no depth, there were no distances, and Joško rolled and twisted and dove, his head struck a stone and in the darkness were cubes of light, blue and white and shale-gray. The cubes swarmed and converged, collided and shattered, and the fragments glittered as they rained into the black below.

He arched back to the surface, gasped, and opened his one good eye. The head of Hadžihafizbegović was floating alongside him, smiling serenely. Joško swam as fast as he could with the light current, hoping that he was invisible.

He looked back, and the head was still following. The river widened and the water grew shallow again. He staggered to his feet and took the earring from his pocket. He waited, grabbed the head from the water, held it to his chest and tried to put the earring into the remaining ear, but it slipped from his hand and was lost. He threw the head onto the shore. It rolled back into the water and bobbed gently toward him.

He lunged away and the head stayed with him, the mouth laughing now, and one eye winked obscenely. Joško dove again, swam until his air was gone and stones cut at his chest. He thrashed back to the surface, looked around for the head of Hadžihafizbegović, and did not see it anywhere.

He pulled himself onto the bank to rest. On the far side of the river there was a single willow, and as he watched, the tree became his sister. Klara called to him, stripped off her long dress and walked into the water. He met her midstream, and as they swam they grew younger and younger until they were children again, and their mother was waving to them from the near bank. She held flowers, perhaps for the graves of his friends now at peace, and from somewhere he heard the music of his father's mandolin spinning and rippling in the air. He and Klara swam faster and faster, and his mother disappeared as they rounded a bend. His father's music faded, and his sister came to him, kissed him and dove and was gone.

Joško got to his feet and began walking but stayed in the river—he knew that he could never again leave the water. Overhead the sun reached in all directions, and the moon hung near the horizon, needle-thin and waiting.

He closed his good eye, and walking in that darkness was a comfort, a way to be safe. He walked and fell, got up and kept walking. The darkness went darker, he opened his eye, and above him was a bridge hovering over the water like the wing of a giant bird. He came out from under it, and to his right was a vineyard, the vines twisting in the faint wind. To his left was a man standing knee-deep in the river, holding a bottle in each hand. The man smiled or frowned. Joško looked past him and saw other men, a massive oak, a terrace, a low white building. The men became ogres, hunched and gnarled. Joško shivered and clutched and fell.

The water took him in, held him close, and bubbles left his mouth, pinpricks of light and crystal globes that vanished into the surface. There was no pain, no trouble of any kind, just the rushing water full in his ears. He settled on the bottom, and the current drew his arms out and away from his body, and the liquid mirror above reflected nothing.

There was a flurry of white, and he was wrenched up through the surface to the light that scalded and froze. Two men were at his sides, lifting him, and Joško fought them off, but now they weren't ogres, they were clowns, and it was all a tremendous game. He patted one of them on the head and snatched the bulbous red nose of the other, laughed at how they shied and stumbled in the water. He splashed at them, but they did not splash back. They came to him again, he fell and rose and the men were not clowns but mercenaries. He pulled away but now they were priests and they beckoned him toward the bank.

The priests began to whisper, forgiving him for whatever he had done. He let himself be guided onto the sand, and now he could forgive as well: the Serb jets and Magarac, the soldiers on the road to Dubrovnik, the men at the dam and the ax on the old man's shoulder. The priests took him up past the oak to the terrace of the white building, and Joško didn't want to go, but surely the priests knew what was best. Then a river of words flowed into his mind, one last special mission, and he sang to all who would listen.

Acknowledgments and Thanks

For love: Ana Lucía Nieto de Kesey.

For, among other things, deft suggestions: Pat Rushin, Sue Henderson, John Leary, Seth Shafer, Kevin Dolgin, Xujun Eberlein, Eric Abrahamsen, Jacquie Woodruff, Jonathan Posen.

Also for love: Tom and Jane Kesey, Kelly and Dave Clark.

For technical and various other forms of support: Maria Massie, Terry Bain, Igor Kajari, Nick Otto, Jim Morris, Francis Ford Coppola, Berthana Bonsang, Sibyl MacKenzie, Rob Krott.

For bringing me things made of paper and sequins and glue: Chloë Kesey, Thomas Kesey.

For permission to reprint the parts of this book which first appeared in slightly different forms in their splendid magazines: the editors at Opium and The Florida Review.

For many things: Jim Ruland.

For many, many others things: Ivana Širović and her family.

Also by Roy Kesey:
All Over

Roy Kesey is the author of the short story collection *All Over*. His work has appeared in *McSweeney's, The Kenyon Review* and *American Short Fiction*, among other magazines, as well as in *Best American Short Stories 2007, New Sudden Fiction 2006* and the *Robert Olen Butler Prize Anthology*. He currently lives in Beijing with his wife and children.